Jack Chabrol Entered The Room.

Jessica's first thought was that he hadn't changed at all. Tall and powerfully built, he still gave the impression of dwarfing those around him. His black hair was cut shorter than he had worn it then. The light brown eyes were still heavily lashed, direct, and an unusual amber cast.

The features hadn't changed: the bold straight nose, the finely molded mouth with its full, sensual lower lip, and the cleft chin of his Norman ancestors. He was still handsome, still overwhelming—still, indisputedly, Jack.

The lawyer stepped forward to introduce them.

"Miss Portman and I are already acquainted. We were at school together," he said coolly, his expression revealing nothing.

Jessica had no recourse but to shake his hand, which she did briefly. His eyes betrayed him, flickering at her touch. She stepped back, thinking how their positions had reversed since they'd last met and hoping he could not hear the blood pounding in her ears.

Dear Reader,

Welcome to Silhouette! Our goal is to give you hours of unbeatable reading pleasure, and we hope you'll enjoy each month's six new Silhouette Desires. These sensual, provocative love stories are both believable and compelling—sometimes they're poignant, sometimes humorous, but always enjoyable.

Indulge yourself. Experience all the passion and excitement of falling in love along with our heroine as she meets the irresistible man of her dreams and together they overcome all obstacles in the path to a happy ending.

If this is your first Desire, I hope it'll be the first of many. If you're already a Silhouette Desire reader, thanks for your support! Look for some of your favorite authors in the coming months: Stephanie James, Diana Palmer, Dixie Browning, Ann Major and Doreen Owens Malek, to name just a few.

Happy reading!

Isabel Swift
Senior Editor

SDRL-7/85

DOREEN OWENS MALEK
Bright River

Silhouette Desire

Published by Silhouette Books New York

America's Publisher of Contemporary Romance

SILHOUETTE BOOKS
300 East 42nd St., New York, N.Y. 10017

Copyright © 1987 by Doreen Owens Malek

ISBN: 0-373-05343-6

First Silhouette Books printing April 1987

America's Publisher of Contemporary Romance

Printed in the U.S.A.

Books by Doreen Owens Malek

Silhouette Romance

The Crystal Unicorn #363

Silhouette Special Edition

A Ruling Passion #154

Silhouette Desire

Native Season #86
Reckless Moon #222
Winter Meeting #240
Desperado #260
Firestorm #290
Bright River #343

Silhouette Intimate Moments

The Eden Tree #88
Devil's Deception #105
Montega's Mistress #169

DOREEN OWENS MALEK

is an attorney and former teacher who decided on her current career when she sold her fledgling novel to the first editor who read it. She has been writing ever since. Born and raised in New Jersey, she has lived throughout the Northeast and now makes her home in Pennsylvania.

One

___

Bright River in autumn was a beautiful place. During her absence Jessica Portman had often remembered its fall glory, and now she was not disappointed by the reality. October filled the sky with brilliant morning sunlight and the lawns and gutters with rainbow bundles of fallen leaves. The trees, shedding amber and russet and gold, were still laden, but Jessica knew that in a few weeks they would be bare and wintry, portents of the cold months to come. The "sere season" was brief in western Massachusetts, short but memorable, a kaleidoscope of color contrasting sharply with the whiteness of the ensuing snow. As Jessica drove her rented car down Main Street, she noticed the changes that the passing of the years had wrought: a brick front on the corner pharmacy, a bakery where the hardware store had once been, new branches of the bank and post office in a tiny mall fronting the road. But despite the additions, there was an air of seediness and disrepair about Bright River that had been absent the last time Jessica was home. She was painfully aware of the reason for the change in the community, because it had also occasioned her return. The Portman mill was failing, and the town was failing with it.

At the intersection, Jessica turned left toward the water onto Walnut Street. She could see the gleaming river in the distance, and the gray bulk of the mill hugging its banks. The office of her father's lawyer was at the end of the street, and she pulled into the parking lot with a strong sense of foreboding, conscious of the fact that the coming interview would not be pleasant. Her father was gravely ill, deep in debt, and his business was being absorbed by a rival company that had gradually been buying up its shares. The once flourishing mill, now in serious trouble, had been ruined by the competitor buying it, and it was Jessica's grim task to handle the final transfer. Her father was hospitalized, and her sister was still too young to take an active role in the crisis that had brought Jessica back from her job in Italy.

She locked her car and entered the office through a glass front door. Inside, the carpeting was a different color but Jason Ransom was the same, as gray and groomed as Jessica remembered him. He came out of his office as the young secretary, a clone of the one he'd had ten years earlier, looked up at Jessica inquiringly.

"It's all right, Laurie, I'll take care of Miss Portman," Ransom said warmly, nodding at the young woman and extending his hand to Jessica. He smiled engagingly, displaying the expensive dental work George Portman had partially financed with his account. "How nice to see you after so long, Jessica. You look wonderful," Ransom went on, as Jessica shook his hand and allowed him to lead her into his paneled sanctum, which was lined with books. "I only wish this meeting was under happier circumstances. How is your father today?"

"Holding his own, they tell me, whatever that means. He's still in the intensive care unit, and they won't allow any visitors until he's well enough to go into a regular room."

"I see," Ransom said as he pulled out a chair for her at the conference table and then sat opposite her. "I was hoping for better news. Your father and I are old friends."

"Yes, Mr. Ransom, I know, and I want to thank you for all the work you've done preparing this transaction."

"I think you're old enough to call me Jason now," the lawyer replied, smiling. "And don't thank me until the deal is made. I doubt if you'll realize much cash. The outstanding bills were quite a bit worse than I thought."

"Anything will help. I'm trying to save the house and get together enough for my sister Jean's tuition next year."

The lawyer's expression told her that both tasks would be formidable.

"When will the takeover be complete?" Jessica asked miserably, dreading the answer.

"Very soon," the lawyer replied. "As you know, JC Enterprises has been undercutting your father's prices for several years now, importing yarn to keep costs down and then pricing the fabric lower for the wholesalers. At the same time, the company has been buying Portman stock until, at this point, it is about to become the major shareholder."

"Isn't there anything at all that can be done?"

Ransom sighed. "What it boils down to is this: either your father accepts the inevitable, bails out and takes what little is left, or he is ruined completely."

"I see," Jessica said hopelessly. JC Enterprises had done a very thorough job. "What's the story with this takeover company?" she asked.

"It's a diversified firm, into trucking mostly, but with some interests in other areas. It's owned by a local boy who made good and came back to his old stamping grounds to set up shop. Maybe you've heard of him. He used to play pro football. Jack Chabrol."

Jessica could not prevent her reaction to the name from showing on her face. As the shock waves receded she heard Ransom saying, "Jessica, are you all right? You've gone white, my dear. You look positively ill. Do you want a drink of water?"

He was about to move toward the door when Jessica raised her hand to stop him. It was a moment before she could trust herself to speak.

"I'm fine, Jason, just give me a minute. I felt a bit faint. I guess I shouldn't have skipped breakfast." She smiled wanly, trying to dispel his alarm, but the attempt wasn't terribly successful. The older man continued to hover until she waved him back into his seat. "Go on, Jason, I'm anxious to hear the details. Tell me the rest."

"Well, it appears that Chabrol has had this move in mind for some while, patiently taking over a little at a time, until now he's ready to acquire the shares that will make him the major shareholder. This was all sub rosa, nothing's been leaked about the change of hands. It wasn't in the papers, you know. I thought it best to handle it privately to spare your family the, uh, embarrassment."

"I understand," Jessica said, beginning to regain her equilibrium. "You did the right thing."

"And as for the workers, well, it wouldn't be a good idea if the news got out about a new owner while the deal was still pending."

Jessica folded her trembling hands. "Tell me about Chabrol," she said calmly.

Ransom raised his brows. "Oh, he went to school here, became a football star, then went to college on a scholarship and was recruited for the pros. He played for about four years until an injury retired him, then he came back to town and started his trucking outfit with the money he'd made. His parents worked in your father's mill, as a matter of fact." He stopped and frowned. "He's about your age. Don't you remember him?"

"I remember him," Jessica responded softly. "But he was a little older. We weren't in the same year. And I left town before I finished high school, if you recall." Her fingers knotted in her lap, and she swallowed, avoiding the lawyer's eyes.

"Yes, I do," Ransom said slowly, his expression thoughtful. Jessica waited, alert to any change in his manner, but he merely picked up a file and began to leaf through it. She expelled her breath noiselessly, rising from her seat. He hadn't heard any gossip, then, any rumors, or if he had he'd forgotten them. One thing was certain: her father hadn't taken Ransom into his confidence, or the lawyer would be aware of the situation developing under his nose. Jessica walked to the window at the back of the room, staring out at the glorious day, trying to absorb this unexpected development.

"I have the proposal in writing right here, if you'd care to see it," Ransom said, rattling a sheet of paper. "It's not a legally binding contract. I thought you'd like to meet with Chabrol before we drew up the papers. He should be here in a few minutes."

It was a good thing Jessica's back was to him, or she would have given the lawyer more cause for concern. She closed her eyes, swaying on her feet, praying for control.

How could this be happening? Within minutes of her arrival, she had learned not only that the takeover company was Jack Chabrol's, but that its owner was about to appear at any moment. It was like a nightmare.

"I hadn't expected to see him so soon," Jessica managed to say after a long moment, remaining at the window, playing for time.

"I thought you wanted to wrap this up as quickly as possible," Ransom replied, confused. "You said you had to get back to your job."

Jessica turned to face him apologetically. "Of course, Jason, I'm sorry. It's just that so much has been happening. Between flying in from Europe, dealing with my father's illness and handling this crisis, I feel at the center of a whirlwind. It's a lot to tackle at once."

Ransom instantly became the concerned protector. "Don't worry about the deal," he said soothingly. "Chabrol is ready to move. It's almost worked out. This won't be difficult."

Jessica almost laughed out loud, restraining herself with an effort. Difficult. What a joke.

The intercom on Ransom's desk buzzed, and he got up to answer it. He pressed a button. "Yes?"

"Mr. Chabrol is here," the secretary announced.

Jessica felt her heart begin to pound. He was in the office, on the other side of that wall.

"Send him in," Ransom said, and Jessica braced herself, literally, putting her hand behind her to grasp the windowsill.

The door opened, and Jack Chabrol entered the room. He looked past Ransom as if the lawyer weren't there, his eyes seeking Jessica's and holding them. He didn't say a word, but he didn't have to.

Jessica's first thought was that he hadn't changed at all. Tall and powerfully built, he still gave the impression of dwarfing those around him. His height had been most arresting in the youth she remembered. His black hair was cut shorter than he had worn it, layered from the center in a current style rather than parted on the side. The light brown eyes were still heavily lashed, direct, with an amber cast that distinguished them from ordinary eyes. The features hadn't changed: the bold, straight nose; the finely molded mouth with its full, sensual lower lip; and the cleft chin of his Norman ancestors. He was still handsome, still overwhelming, still, indisputably, Jack.

He turned his head a little and looked at her out of the corner of his eye. It was a gesture uniquely his, and ten years earlier it had had the power to stop her heart. Jessica discovered, with a sinking feeling of dismay, that it still did. She took a breath, looking her fill. She could now see the fine lines bracketing his eyes and mouth, the assured carriage of his dark head and the authority in his manner. The boy she had known was gone, replaced by this purposeful, enigmatic stranger.

Ransom cleared his throat, obviously wondering what the hell was going on between his two clients, who were staring at each other like combatants in an O'Neill play. Jack glanced at him, as if remembering his presence.

"Ransom," he said in greeting, and his voice was older, like the rest of him.

The lawyer stepped forward. "Jessica, allow me to introduce..." he began.

Jack crossed the distance between him and Jessica, extending his hand.

"Miss Portman and I are acquainted. We were at school together," he said coolly, his expression revealing nothing.

Jessica had no recourse but to shake hands, which she did briefly. His eyes betrayed him, flickering at her touch, but his slight smile was distant, professional.

"You look very well," he said evenly.

"Thank you. So do you," Jessica replied, and meant it. Prosperity sat upon his shoulders, and he wore it with aplomb. His navy wool suit was impeccably tailored, obviously expensive, and his light blue oxford shirt looked custom made. His striped tie was silk, his watch was Rolex and the Bally loafers on his feet shone like shipboard brass. She stepped back, thinking how their positions had reversed since they'd last met and hoping that he could not hear the blood pounding in her ears.

The intercom buzzed again, and they both looked toward it, startled by the intrusion on what was, to them, a private tableau.

"I'm sorry to interrupt," the secretary said, "but the messenger from Crowley and Dodd is here. Mr. Dodd thinks the Henley contract is still wrong, and he sent a note..."

Ransom sighed. "I'll be right out, Laurie. Tell the boy to wait." He turned to his companions. "Please excuse me. I'll settle this and be back shortly."

"Take your time," Jack said, and Jessica thought she detected an undertone of malice in the pleasantry. She would be left alone with him, and he was looking forward to it.

As Ransom went through the door, Jack turned to her and his eyes raked her, freed of the restraint the lawyer's presence had imposed. He was unsmiling now, all traces of surface politeness gone. His mouth looked set in granite.

"Hello, Jesse," he said softly, his tone belying the hard glint in his eyes. It was as if the first greeting had never taken place.

Jessica flinched inwardly. He was coming out of the corner swinging, all right. From childhood, her imperious father had insisted that everyone call her by her full name, and everyone had. Everyone, that is, except Jack. To him, and only him, she had always been Jesse.

"Hello, Jack."

"You're as beautiful as ever," he said finally, after several moments of study. "I wondered if you would be."

"Were you hoping I had turned into a hag?" Jessica asked lightly, feeling dizzy, as if on the edge of a precipice.

"I never thought there was much chance of that," he replied shortly, sounding almost resentful. He had known that God would fail to punish her, and that, like Dorian Gray, she would remain fresh and unmarked while concealing within her a stained and guilty soul.

"But you do seem . . . upset," he added smoothly, offering what was surely the understatement of the year.

"I'm worried about my father," she said shortly.

"Still beautiful," he murmured, his eyes narrowing slightly, "and still a liar."

So much for the attempt at civilized conversation.

"You have the advantage in this," she said, looking away from the probing intensity of his gaze. "You were prepared to see me. I didn't know who JC Enterprises was until this morning."

"Surely you weren't surprised?" he asked. The sentence was almost a sneer.

"At first. I knew you were no longer playing football, but I hadn't realized that you'd returned to town." She paused. "So you were behind this all along, Jack."

He faced her down, his expression glacial. "That's right."

"You plotted this like a general devising a military campaign." She paused and then whispered, "Was it really necessary to go this far?"

"I thought so," he replied tightly.

"No half measures for you. Right, Jack?" she said quietly.

He didn't answer, and she remembered that about him. He didn't fight, he didn't argue, and he didn't debate. He put up a stony wall of silence when crossed or contradicted, and it could be maddening.

"Now you have your revenge, on my father and me. For the past," she went on.

He was saved from replying by Ransom's return. The lawyer began to talk about the details of the sale, and as she listened to Jack's comments, she realized that his speech had changed. His accent, so pronounced when he was younger, was almost gone, and she missed it. Now he sounded like an English-language news announcer in his native Quebec—lilting, slightly nasal, but no longer really French.

"And we'll have a complete inventory of the assets ready by Friday," Ransom was saying. "I'd like for us to get together then to go over the list and the estimates for the machine repairs. How does that sound to you, Jessica?"

"All right," she said, thinking that she would get the whole thing over with today if she could.

"Here's a copy of the file, as you requested," Ransom added, handing Jack a manila folder. "You can have your people look it over and get back to me with any questions, but I think you'll find that everything is in order. Jessica, do you have something to add?"

"No."

Jack glanced at her. "May I give you a lift anywhere?" he asked neutrally.

"No, thank you. I have a car." He must have known she would never go with him; the offer was for Ransom's benefit.

"I'll see both of you on Friday, then," Jack said in parting and shook hands again with Ransom, nodding in Jessica's direction. She didn't breathe easily until he had left the room.

"Quite a personable young man," Ransom commented, pleased with the proceedings. "I think this is going to work out very well."

Speak for yourself, Jessica thought darkly. She got to her feet and said, "Will there be much of anything left over for me to hold things together?"

Ransom sighed. "I can't promise that, Jessica, we'll have to see what Chabrol does when the final inventory is in. As I said, his takeover bid was just preliminary, and these figures can change by a substantial margin when you take into account goodwill for the wholesalers and the amount of unfinished product on hand. We'll just have to wait and hope for the best."

Jessica nodded dismally, thinking that her fate was now in the hands of the last person on earth who would wish her well. She saw it as irony; to Jack it must seem like poetic justice.

As she headed for the door, Ransom said, "I'll call you to set up the meeting. And try not to worry. I'll do my best for you, and this Chabrol seems like a decent sort. I think the final resolution will be fair."

He could not know how little that observation comforted her, but she appreciated his good intentions. "Thanks, Jason. For everything."

"I'll be in touch."

Jessica paused outside his office door and asked his secretary if she could use the rest room. The young woman pointed to the appropriate door. Jessica slipped inside the little cubicle and leaned against the wall. It was a relief to be unobserved, to let the mask of composure slip. She glanced in the mirror over the sink, wondering what Jack had thought of her. He had said she was still beautiful, and she tried to achieve a clinical detachment as she surveyed her features in the glass.

Her blond hair had been long in high school, almost to her waist, and he had loved to play with the gossamer strands. It was shorter now, shoulder length, but the almond-shaped green eyes, small straight nose, and wide mouth looked the same. She had the pale prettiness of her Danish mother, and once when she and Jack had gone for a midnight walk he'd called her his *ange d'argent,* his silver angel, because her skin and hair had looked silver in the moonlight.

Jessica's eyes filled, and she allowed herself the luxury of tears. The silver angel was tarnished now, and no amount of polish could ever make her shine again in Jack Chabrol's eyes.

Oh, how she had loved him. She would never love anybody like that again, not as long as she lived. The all-consuming passion of innocence awakened, of youth blossoming into adulthood, happened only once, and she had lost it forever, to her abiding regret.

She blinked and wiped her eyes with a tissue she'd retrieved from the bottom of her purse. When she felt composed enough to drive, she emerged from the bathroom to the puzzled stare of the secretary, who doubtless thought she had been knitting an afghan in there. Jessica glided past her with as much dignity as she could muster, emerging into the October sunshine with relief. She took several deep breaths of the fragrant air, redolent of wood smoke and the fallen apples on Lawson's lawn, and felt better.

She headed for her car, resigned to her fate. She would deal with this because she had to, and then return to the life she had interrupted. Jack Chabrol was part of her past.

Somehow, she must find a way to keep him there.

Jack pulled into the parking space with his name on it and shut off the engine of his car. Before him loomed the impressive expanse of his offices, modern, sparkling with chrome and glass, built on a strip of farmland he had purchased on the outskirts of town. It was the latest, in fact the only, addition to Bright River's economic growth in recent years. His advisers had all told him to build elsewhere, in a more prosperous locale, especially since the bulk of his business came from the industrial towns farther north. But Jack had insisted on returning to the scene of his youth, creating before the staring eyes of the townspeople this monument, the palpable evidence of his success. Today it looked back at him, blank and featureless, small comfort after the trauma of the interview he'd just experienced.

Jack leaned back against the headrest and closed his eyes, seeing again the expression on Jessica's face, a mixture of apprehension and innate pride. She'd looked as if she knew she deserved anything he might do to her, but was going to face it without a whimper. All this time, he'd thought he would want to strike her, or shout at her, do something to make her pay for the cold pain that had lain in his breast for a decade like a rock. But at the sight of her, the gut-wrenching desire had returned, the relentless yearning that had made him defy her father and convention to possess her. So he'd taken refuge in icy politeness, conducting a business deal with the one woman he had never been able to forget.

It was a ludicrous turn of events, but he had himself to thank for that. He'd dedicated the past four years of his life to ruining George Portman, and now he was on the very brink of accomplishing that feat. When it became clear that Jesse would be involved, he'd wanted to see her, talk to her again. He had returned to Bright River two years earlier half hoping to find her there, but had learned that she'd never come back, even though her father and sister still lived in the big house overlooking the river. His sister, Lalage, had heard from Jean Portman that Jesse was divorced, but working in Europe and unlikely to visit the family home. Jack had left the matter there, unwilling to demonstrate a show of interest, but his disappointment at not being able to impress her with his new status was deep and bitter. Now he had his chance; she was back and in trouble. The poor boy had the rich girl at his mercy, the long-sought triumph was about to be his.

The need to hurt her was so strong that it ran through his body like a toxin in his blood. Once Jesse had matched his passion with hers, swearing eternal loyalty and undying devotion. Until she'd disappeared without a word—to marry another man.

Jack sighed and opened the door, turning his mind to the meeting that awaited him inside: contract negotiations with his drivers. It would be difficult to concentrate, but he was grateful for the distraction. Until the session was over, he wouldn't have to think about Jesse again.

Jessica parked in the driveway of her father's house, deciding to leave her luggage in the trunk of the car until later. She had gone to Ransom's office directly from the airport. Now she let herself in with her old key, dull with disuse. Jean was at school, and Jessica prowled the silent halls alone, looking into the rooms on the first floor, changed minimally since she had last seen them. The cherry antiques and bric-a-brac George Portman had inherited from his father furnished the house in a durable style not subject to the whims of fashion. Jessica climbed the central staircase slowly, noticing that the third step creaked, as it always had, and then paused on the landing, looking at the closed door of her room at the end of the hall.

Biting her trembling lower lip, Jessica crossed the Oriental runner on the hardwood floor, faded and worn now with the passage of many feet, and pushed open the paneled oak door.

The room assaulted her with memories, and she almost felt like covering her ears, so real and insistent were the voices she heard: her father's, Jean's first-grade babble, and in the background, fading but still discernible, the soft murmur of her mother. Visually, everything was the same as she had left it. The chintz curtains and spread, the canopy on the four-poster, even the window seat upholstered in the same flowered fabric remained unchanged. There she had sat and dreamed her adolescent dreams, looking over the rooftops toward the ribbon of the river. The site of the house, on a height above the town, had been chosen for its view, and sitting at the top of the house in this curtained bower, she had felt mistress of all she surveyed.

Jessica shook her head sadly, knowing how wrong she had been. That last winter, when she was four months shy of her eighteenth birthday, everything had fallen apart. She had left this room and this house, and until today she had not returned.

She went to the window and crept onto the seat, folding her legs under her and leaning her head against the frame. What would I give to change the past? she wondered. To go back to that year and do everything over again, make it come out right this time? She closed her eyes and gave in to the rush of memory, so long suppressed, which, like the flood from a bursting dam, washed over and engulfed her.

Two

Jessica was ten when her sister, Jean, was born. Her mother died shortly after having the baby, and George Portman soon discovered that he could not care for two children by himself. He hired a nanny for Jean and sent Jessica to boarding school, which left him free to pursue the consuming interest of his life: running his business. Jessica remained away, except for brief vacations, even spending summers at camp, until she developed mononucleosis during her sophomore year of high school. At first she was treated for flu in the infirmary, but when she did not improve, the headmistress called in a specialist, who diagnosed the problem. Concerned about the long-term nature of the illness, the doctor felt that Jessica should probably go home to recuperate. The principal passed this recommendation on to Jessica's father, who sent for his daughter.

Portman engaged a nurse to care for her, and all through that spring and summer Jessica languished in bed, forbidden to do anything other than read and watch television. The treatment consisted of little more than rest and proper diet, and once she felt better she became restless, eager to get up and resume her life. She studied at home and took make-up exams to complete her courses. By August blood tests indicated that her red cells had returned to normal, and she was pronounced fit to resume her education.

But George Portman was convinced that her previous school had neglected Jessica's health and decided to keep her at home. He enrolled her in the Bright River regional high school, where she began her junior year in the fall.

For the first time in her life Jessica was exposed to the atmosphere of a coeducational public school. The transition from the uniformed young ladies of her boarding school past to the denim clad students who surrounded her now was a thrilling and heady experience. She was accustomed to being in class with girls, even if they dressed and behaved quite differently, but the boys! She couldn't get used to their size, their voices, their constantly felt masculine presence. They seemed to be everywhere, large and muscular with coltish bodies and shining, shaggy hair, talking and laughing, lounging indolently in doorways and watching her with covetous, curious eyes.

Was it because she was George Portman's daughter that she drew so much attention? She thought so, not realizing that most of them didn't know who she was, but were attracted to the new, pretty blonde in their midst. When she was identified, sometimes she was resented, as the children of mill hands comprised a large portion of the student body. But as time passed, her natural, unassuming personality caused those who might have held her parentage against her to forget about it, and Jessica began to blend in and adjust.

She had been in the school for almost a month and had made a friend, when something happened to change her life. The friend was Madeline Conway, whose father ran the delivery service for Portman Mills. Jessica had known Madeline previously, from some company picnics and Christmas parties she'd attended, but when the girls discovered they were in the same homeroom their acquaintance ripened and they became close. Maddy, as she was called, was outgoing and chatty, Jessica's unofficial tour guide. When Jessica had a question or wanted to inquire about some procedure or regulation, Maddy was sure to know the answer.

One day at the beginning of their lunch period, Maddy and Jessica were standing at the latter's locker when Jessica felt a pair of eyes on her. The staring persisted while she put her books on the shelves, until she finally became uncomfortable enough to turn and look. She met the gaze of a tall, broad shouldered dark boy in a senior letterman's jacket. Instead of turning away, flustered at being caught, he continued to look at her steadily, completely unruffled by her awareness of him.

Jessica glanced away, but then was drawn back to him. He was still looking, his serious, thoughtful expression oddly mature and definitely unnerving. They remained that way, locked in silent communication across the crowded corridor, until another student touched the boy's shoulder and he turned. Jessica looked back at Maddy, who was observing the scene with interest.

"What was that about?" she asked Jessica, nodding toward the dark boy, who was now walking off after casting a departing glance over his shoulder.

"That guy was staring at me," Jessica replied.

Maddy smiled slyly. "Don't you know who that is?"

Jessica shook her head, slamming her locker door closed with a bang.

"Only the bad actor of the football team, that's who," Maddy said with relish, obviously enjoying her role of knowledgeable informant. "Jack Chabrol. His real name is Jacques—don't you love it? He's a senior and his family is from Canada, you know, the French province. He has this terrific accent, you should hear him. They just moved here about three years ago. There's a sister in ninth and a bunch of little kids running around. He lives in that old brick tenement down by the river."

"Too bad you don't know anything about him," Jessica commented dryly.

"Hey, I make it my business to find out these things. I'm surprised you weren't aware of him. His parents work in your dad's factory."

That gave Jessica a moment's pause. Her father was notorious for using cheap immigrant labor, and apparently the Chabrols were part of his underpaid work force.

"He's suspended from the team right now," Maddy rambled on, "but he'll be reinstated soon. The coach needs him too much to bench him for long. He had a fight with the captain, Jeff Thompson, when Jeff tossed off some remark about his family."

"His family?"

"Yeah, Jeff was making fun of the way they talk, or something."

"Oh," Jessica said thoughtfully.

"Cute, isn't he?" Maddy asked, nudging Jessica in the ribs.

"I didn't notice," Jessica sniffed, but her barely suppressed smile gave her away.

"Hah," Maddy said derisively. "You'd have to be dead not to notice, and at last check you were very much alive."

"I *will* be dead if I flunk this trig quiz," Jessica said, deliberately changing the subject.

"I got a fifty on the last one," Maddy said gloomily. "At this rate I'll be thirty-five before I graduate from high school."

Jessica continued the conversation about the upcoming test, but her mind was on the encounter that had just taken place. Whether she would admit it to her friend or not, she knew that from now on, as she passed through the corridors of Bright River High, she would be looking for a certain face in the crowd.

On the following afternoon, Jessica was sitting in last period study when Jack Chabrol sauntered through the double doors of the auditorium. He flashed a hall pass at the monitor, Miss Chambers, who barely glanced at it and waved him toward the sea of students. Last period was an "open" study hall, which meant that it was a catchall for those kids who weren't scheduled for a class, and people wandered freely in and out of it, frequently excused for student council meetings, team practices and other activities. Jessica watched, her heart beating faster, as Jack approached and slipped into the empty seat behind her.

"Hi," he said into her ear, as Miss Chambers shifted a stack of papers on her desk and bent her head again.

When Jessica didn't answer he added, "I saw you in the hall at lunch yesterday."

Miss Chambers continued to scribble, so Jessica turned her head and whispered, "You've never been in this study before."

"That's true. I have a standing excuse for football practice, but I'm suspended from the team for a while."

Maddy was right about his accent. When he said, "That's true," the first word came out as "Zat's," and Jessica thought it was delightful.

"So," he went on. "You're new, aren't you? I would have remembered you from last year."

"I transferred in from private school in September."

Miss Chambers looked up and sent them both the death ray. Jessica dropped her eyes to her book.

Silence reigned for several minutes, and then a folded note dropped over Jessica's shoulder and onto her desk. She shoved it under her hand until Miss Chambers was completely absorbed, and then opened it to read: "Meet me by the flagpole after the last bell. I'll wait."

Jessica shifted in her seat and looked at Jack fully for the first time. At close range his brown eyes were flecked with gold, and he had a small scar, long ago faded to white, at the base of his chin, just below the cleft. She nodded, and he smiled.

That was the beginning.

On their first date Jessica insisted on meeting Jack at the movies. He dismissed her reluctance to have him come to her house philosophically; lots of girls had difficult parents. But when she wanted to walk home alone, he was determined to accompany her, and it wasn't until they arrived at their destination that he understood the reason for her behavior. He hadn't asked Jessica's last name because he didn't care what it was, but he did know the owner of the imposing colonial on the knoll at the edge of town. When Jessica paused in front of it and turned to face him, he released her hand, his expression changing.

"This is your house?" he asked quietly.

"Yes."

"Old man Portman is your father?"

"Yes." Then, unable to stop herself, she added anxiously, "Does it matter?"

"Does it matter to you?" Jack countered.

"No."

"But we both know it will to your dad," he went on, and Jessica couldn't disagree. Portman's reputation was widespread and well deserved. He regarded Bright River as his private fiefdom, and Jessica as his inviolate property. It went without saying that the son of two of his factory workers would not be considered an appropriate companion for his daughter. And Portman was not one to stand idly by and let his child pursue her own course. If he discovered that Jessica was seeing Jack, there would be a price to pay.

"This is why you didn't want me to pick you up tonight," Jack said flatly.

Jessica looked away.

"How long did you think you could keep it a secret?" Jack asked. "Somebody at school was sure to tell me, or I would have seen your name. This just happened so fast that I didn't think..."

"That I might be the daughter of the least popular man in town," Jessica finished miserably.

Jack put his arm around her shoulders and pulled her against his chest. They didn't talk for a long moment and then he said, his lips against her hair, "If I did go to meet him, would he throw me out?"

"I don't know what he would do. I can't think about it," Jessica murmured, closing her eyes and pressing her cheek to his sweater. "I'm sorry," she added softly. "I know it's horribly unfair."

"Oh, I understand," Jack said bitterly. "Certainly a serf like me is not fit company for George Portman's little princess. And I'm a Canuck who can't speak proper English to boot. Your father would probably have me shot."

"Don't talk about yourself that way."

"It's true, isn't it? He didn't spend a fortune sending you to those fancy schools in order to have you hang out with me." Jack made a disgusted sound and added, "How could I have been so stupid? I should have realized before this what the situation was." He paused. "Maybe we shouldn't see each other anymore."

Jessica drew back from him and looked into his face. "Is that what you want?" she whispered.

In answer, he pulled her back into his arms. They had only known each other a short time, but it was already clear to them that their developing relationship was too important to surrender to circumstances.

"Maybe I should just pick you up some night and introduce myself," Jack said desperately, clearly preferring the confrontational approach to the other one available to them: sneaking around and meeting in secret.

Jessica demurred. "No, Jack," she said sadly. "You have to consider your parents' jobs."

"You think he would fire them?" Jack said, aghast. It seemed an extreme reaction to a disobedient daughter's dating choice.

Jessica, who knew her father, considered it a strong possibility. "He once got rid of a cook we had because she used to bring her little girl to work and he caught me playing with her a couple of times."

Jack received this disclosure with a long silence. Then he said, stroking Jessica's hair absently, "We'll just have to be careful, that's all. Keep a low profile at school, so word doesn't get back to your father. It's good that we haven't been together much so far. I don't think we've attracted much attention."

"Maddy knows, but she won't say anything." A note of humor crept into Jessica's tone. "Won't it seem odd that you don't have some girl clinging to your arm everywhere you go? I've heard that was your usual practice in the past."

"Never a girl like you," he said quietly.

"What do you mean?"

He looked at her as though she were speaking a foreign language. "Nice girls don't go out with me; don't you know that yet?"

"Why not?"

He smiled derisively. "It may have something to do with my dear daddy's drinking habits," he answered sarcastically. Then they both shrank back into the shadows as the porch light went on above them.

"Who is it?" Jack murmured, his lips next to Jessica's ear.

"My father locking up." They waited until the light went off again, and then Jack said, "Where does he think you are tonight?"

"At Maddy's house. I told her that if he called there she should say I had gone to the library to pick up a book we needed for our homework."

"Does he usually check up on you?"

"Usually." Jessica sighed, and Jack considered the enormity of the task before him. A small rational voice warned him that he should cut this girl loose and run, but it was easily drowned out by the clarion call of his emotions, which urged him to pursue her. Moderation was not in his vocabulary or in his genes. What he wanted he went after and got, and Jessica would not be an exception.

"You'd better go inside," he said, turning her face up to examine it in the glow from a streetlight.

"Okay." She smiled as he touched her cheek and then released her.

Jessica astonished him by stepping back and diving into the bushes bordering the sidewalk, after a moment coming up with a book pack in her hands. "I stashed this on the way out," she explained. "I couldn't go to Maddy's for a study session without the props."

Jack grinned. "What a woman."

Jessica curtsied. "Thank you."

They became serious again as Jessica shouldered the pack and Jack reached for her hand. He entwined his fingers with hers and said, "I'll meet you on Monday after third period in 301. Mr. Markel leaves the room open, and it's always empty. All right?"

"Okay."

Jack wanted very much to kiss her, but wasn't sure what her response would be. The timing and the location weren't what he would have chosen. As he hesitated, Jessica made the decision for him, standing on tiptoe and touching her lips to his cheek. Not one to miss such an opportunity, Jack turned his head and captured her mouth with his. When she didn't pull away, he put his hands on her shoulders and drew her closer, opening her lips with his tongue. She gasped, and he let her go, crashing back to earth with a thud. Her inexperience was obvious; she hadn't a clue what she was doing. And yet that one brief embrace was to haunt him all his life, remaining in his mind like the refrain of a nostalgic song: the first time he kissed Jesse.

"Good night," she whispered, turning toward the house.

"Good night," he echoed as he watched her cross the lawn and unlock the side door. She glanced back at him, waved and disappeared inside. He stayed a moment longer, aware that something of singular importance had just taken place. Then he put his hands in his pockets and headed home, his thoughts on Monday, when he would see her again.

October and November passed quickly, as time always does for people who are falling in love. Jack and Jessica grew remarkably adept at keeping their relationship a secret, frequently using Maddy, who reveled in the romance of the situation, as a go-between. They met often in school and at school-sponsored activities, and occasionally managed trips out of town in Jack's thirdhand car. They were blissfully happy, despite their uncertain circumstances. Jessica deliberately did not consider what might happen in the future; she lived in the present and cherished every day. She and Jack rarely discussed the necessity for caution or for pretending that they were casual acquaintances when others were around. They just did what they had to do and tried to forget why they were doing it. And that autumn, they seemed to lead a charmed life, engrossed in each other and oblivious to the outside world that might intrude upon them at any moment.

One weekend just before Thanksgiving, Jessica's father returned early from a business trip and found his house deserted. He had taken a taxi from the airport and called upstairs to see if he could locate his daughter. Jessica had told him that she would be studying for a midterm the whole time he was gone. He telephoned Madeline, whose mother said she was at swim practice, and then spent the afternoon and evening wondering if his child had lied to him. Finally he called the home where Jean was spending the night, and Jessica was not there, either. It grew late, and Portman wondered if he should alert the police. He knew that he was probably overreacting, but dealing with his children had never been easy for him. He had married

in his forties, and now, approaching sixty, he was the sole
custodian of a pair of girls he could neither understand nor
control. Jean was a seven-year-old enigma, lost in a world
of crayons and show-and-tell, and Jessica was a blossoming woman who terrified him with her potential for all
sorts of problems. He was standing in the living room,
considering what to do, when he heard a car in the driveway. He went to the window and watched a badly abused,
twelve-year-old Ford pull up to the side door. It stopped in
the glare of the security floodlights on the overhang. His
daughter got out on the passenger side as the driver, a tall,
dark-haired boy with an athlete's build came around and
embraced her, pinning her against the side of the car with
a kiss that transfixed Portman, standing unseen behind the
heavy draperies.

His jaw hardened as the boy finally released her and
Jessica headed for the house, glancing longingly over her
shoulder as she did so. Portman heard her key in the lock
as the car started up again. He walked slowly toward the
hall, his fists bunching with frustration and barely checked
anger. He knew the kid who had just been manhandling
his daughter. He had seen him around the factory a few
times. No wonder Jessica had concealed the obviously intimate relationship. He would put a stop to this. Right
now.

Jessica came through the door, humming under her
breath, and then stopped short when she saw her father
blocking her path. She blanched, almost dropping the keys
in her hand, and then regarded him silently, bracing herself for the first volley.

"I thought you said you would be studying all weekend," he began quietly.

"I thought you said you would be gone until Sunday
night," she countered, her chin coming up.

She was going to be difficult, he saw. No tears or pleas for forgiveness—that was Jean's style. Jessica faced the enemy and fired back. She might cry from sorrow or sadness, but never in combat.

"The conference ended early. Do you have any explanation for the scene I just witnessed through the window?" he said icily, coming directly to the point.

Jessica's shoulders slumped with defeat. So he had seen. She had hoped she could hold him off long enough to come up with a suitable explanation for her absence, but her farewell to Jack required no subtitles. Her father knew it all now, and she waited for the bombs to fall.

"Do you know who that boy is, Jessica?" Portman demanded. "Do you know anything about his family, his background?"

"I know that Jack is a wonderful person..." she interrupted, but Portman cut her short.

"As wonderful as his father, the town drunk? My office manager has bailed Chabrol out of jail several times this year alone. When sober he's the best spinner I've got, which is the reason I haven't fired him, but I will not allow my daughter to keep company with the sort of trash that spends almost as much time in jail as on the job."

"Jack is not trash!" Jessica answered heatedly. "He isn't responsible for his father's problems, and he does everything he can to make up for them. He has two part-time jobs and gives his mother all the money he earns, and he's going to college next year and..."

Portman held up his hand for silence. "I don't want to hear it. I don't care if the boy is about to be knighted. He comes from the gutter and I won't have you joining him there. The family lives in a four-room flat, overrun with filthy, smelly brats. The mother speaks some garbled dia-

lect no one but her children can understand. All of them
run around in rags not fit for a charity collection."

"They can't help it if they're poor," Jessica cried, her
voice full of outrage at his unfairness.

"Jessica, this not a debate. The subject is closed. You
are never to date that boy again. When you see him at
school, you may say hello and goodbye to him, that's all.
If I find that you have disobeyed me, I will arrange for
your transfer to a private school that will make your previous institutions look indulgent. I'll send you as far away
as possible, to France or Switzerland, and the closest you
will get to an adolescent male will be a telephone call from
your cousin Jonathan. Do you understand me, young
lady?"

"I understand," Jessica replied in a subdued tone. Ar-
guing would serve no purpose. "May I go to my room?"

"You may. And I hope you'll find some time to do the
studying you seemed so concerned about when I left on
Friday."

Jessica went upstairs and locked herself in her flowered
retreat, planning her next move. Not for a moment did she
consider obeying her father; the only issue was how to
sustain her relationship with Jack now that Portman knew
about it. After an hour, having formulated a plan, she
emerged from her room and descended the stairs, pausing
in the doorway of her father's study, waiting to be recognized.

Portman looked up from his paperwork and said,
"Yes?"

"I have to call Maddy about a homework assignment."

Her father considered for a moment and then said, "Go
ahead. But make it short. I have to make a few calls."

Jessica went to the hall phone and dialed, wishing for
the hundredth time that her father would allow her to have

an extension in her room. Maddy's younger brother answered and it seemed like an eternity before her friend got to the line and said, "Can't do the trig problems, huh? Me neither."

"Hi, Maddy," Jessica said loudly. "I was wondering if you could tell me what pages we have to read for Mr. Maybury's class."

There was a pause before Maddy answered, "Jessica, what's wrong with you? You sound like you're yelling for the third balcony, and you know Maybury's class has been a study for two weeks since he's been sick."

"That's right," Jessica said. "Was it chapter twelve or thirteen?"

Another pause. Then, "Okay, I get it. I knew something was up when Mom told me your father called here this afternoon, and you had told me he'd be away until tomorrow. Is he listening?"

"Probably."

"Uh-huh, then I'll ask the questions. What do you want me to do?"

"I'd like you to tell that friend of yours, you know the one who's so good in French, that I'd like to borrow her notes."

"You want me to tell Jack something," Maddy said. She was familiar with the routine by now.

"That's right. Tell her that I need to see her."

"When?"

"Tonight," Jessica whispered into the phone, taking a chance. "Three a.m. at the kitchen door. Tell him to walk. The car might be heard."

"Jessica, I need that phone," her father called from the study.

"Right away, Dad," Jessica caroled back to him.

"Three o'clock in the morning?" Maddy said in an incredulous tone. "Are you nuts? It will be twenty degrees at that hour, and your father's home. Can't it wait until Monday?"

"No, it can't," Jessica said in a normal voice. "Will you do that for me?"

"Sure," Maddy said, her shrug coming over the line. "I'll call Jack right now. You'll have to fill me in at school. I can't wait to hear what this is all about. Can you give me a clue?"

"He knows," Jessica said miserably.

"Who knows what? Oh, your father. He knows about Jack."

"Bingo."

"Oh, dear. Well, it had to happen sooner or later. Jessica, are you sure this is a good idea? It's kind of like sending Jack on a suicide mission, isn't it? What if your father wakes up and finds him in your house?"

"Just do it, all right?" Jessica said impatiently as she heard her father rise from his chair in the room behind her. "Thanks a million, got to go. Bye."

She hung up just as Portman emerged from is study. "Phone's all yours," she said politely, and escaped to the second floor.

The night seemed to go on forever. Jessica heard her father go into his room around midnight and waited until two to check on him. She pushed the heavy oak door inward cautiously, formulating an excuse for disturbing him if he should happen to be awake. But he was asleep, curled up on his side, and she exhaled with relief, shutting the door and sneaking along the hall. She passed Jean's room, with its little girl eyelet ruffles and glassy-eyed dolls, and crept down the stairs, taking care to avoid the third from the bottom, which protested loudly at even the slightest weight.

Once in the kitchen, she leaned against the counter with relief, aware that she was shaking. Maddy was right, she was taking an awful chance, but she had to see Jack and share this burden with him, draw sustenance from his strength. He would come, she was sure of it. He would know by the very nature of the request that she was desperate for his company, and it was not in him to deny her.

She watched the street from the window above the sink, and at five to three he came into view, stamping his feet, his gloved hands in the pockets of his football jacket. His breath made a cloud before his face as he glanced up at the house and saw her. He smiled reassuringly, and as she went to the side door to let him in, she already felt better.

As soon as he crossed the threshold he took her in his arms. "Maddy told me," he said into her ear. "How did he find out?"

"He came home early from his trip and saw us outside tonight."

Jack's memory of their parting was vivid, and he was sure it had left nothing to Portman's imagination. "He's asleep upstairs?" he asked, glancing over Jessica's shoulder as if he expected her father to appear at any moment, flaming sword in hand.

Jessica nodded. "Jack, what are we going to do?"

"What did he say?"

"Exactly what I thought he would say."

"You can't see me anymore?"

"That's about the size of it."

"What about at school?"

"'Hello and goodbye.' That's a direct quote."

Jack muttered something in French that Jessica was glad she couldn't understand.

"And he says if I disobey him he'll send me away to school. Really away. Like to Europe," she added.

He pulled back to look into her face, and she could tell that he was worried now. Nothing much frightened Jack, but this did. He knew enough about Jessica's father from her descriptions to believe that he would make good on his threat.

"I'll go to see him," he said impulsively. "He can't be that unreasonable."

Jessica clutched at his hands, dismayed at the resurfacing of his stubborn faith in the merits of communication. "Oh, Jack, don't talk nonsense. He won't listen to you. He'll be enraged that you had the nerve to confront him. He won't see it as two people getting together to talk over a problem, he'll see it as a punk kid defying a responsible, rational adult. He doesn't admire courage, he sees it as a flouting of his will. Don't you understand? You'd get nowhere, and you have to think of your family. Please, promise me you won't try it."

"All right, all right," he murmured, embracing her again and stroking her hair. "We just need time to think. We'll come up with something."

They stood for a few moments in silence, and then Jessica said, "Jack, we have to go upstairs. My father might wake up and come down to the kitchen. We'll lock my door. My room is at the other end of the house. We can talk, and he won't hear us."

"Are you sure?" Jack asked doubtfully.

"Yes, come on," Jessica replied, tugging on his hand. "Sometimes he gets up in the middle of the night and makes a snack." She led him through the house, and he glanced around, impressed. He'd never been inside before, and compared to his parents' home, it was a palace.

At the foot of the stairs Jessica held her finger to her lips and waved him back. He waited in the hall, behind the balustrade and out of sight, while she checked on her father again. The ship's clock on the mantel in the living room ticked ominously, and the house seemed to be full of nocturnal noises, creaks and groans that made him skittish, uneasy. After a moment Jessica leaned over the banister and signaled him to join her. They fled to her room, as silent and light-footed as cats, conspirators who faced certain disaster if discovered.

Once inside her bedroom, Jessica locked the door. Jack stared at the textured wallpaper and sumptuous carpeting, the twin closets, doors ajar, bursting with clothes. The matched furniture was all white and gold, stylized, as pretty and perfect as a doll house. She left this every day to join him, to embrace the drunkard's son and murmur that she loved him? He shook his head. Maybe her father was right.

Jessica turned to face him. "How did you get out tonight?" she asked as he unzipped his jacket, still examining his surroundings.

"My mom is working the night shift. Dad is passed out and the kids are asleep. I think Lalage heard me leaving, but she won't say anything."

Lalage was the eldest girl in the family, the ninth grader Maddy had mentioned. Jack took his jacket off and dropped it on a chair, and then they looked at each other, forced to confront the situation again. Jessica, attired in the floor-length nightgown she had donned to convince her father she was going to bed, appeared so miserable that Jack's only thought was to comfort her. He tapped his lips with two fingers, asking for a kiss, and she flew into his arms.

"Everything is such a mess," she whispered. "I wish I were anyone else, some average girl with a sane father who could live a normal life."

"If you were somebody else I wouldn't love you," he answered, seeking her mouth with his.

Jessica responded immediately, eager to lose the concerns of the moment in lovemaking. It was this state of mind that was their undoing. Always before she had stopped him, pulled away before things went too far, but now their whole relationship was threatened by a force beyond their control. Jack, ever impulsive, even reckless, pressed his advantage, unthinking, conscious only of the yielding woman who clung to him so passionately: Jesse, his Jesse. He lowered her to the bed and fondled her through the folds of the nightdress, his hands seeking and finding softness, curves. He groaned, moving on top of her, and she shifted to accommodate him, gasping as she felt him against her thighs.

He was very strong. Jessica knew that from his prowess on the football field, of course, and from the way he lifted her as if she were made of lemon chiffon, but this was something more. Suddenly, there was nothing boyish about him any longer; he had changed, in the space of seconds, into a man. When he reached for the hem of her gown, she arched her hips to help him, enthralled by their mutual ardor.

Neither one of them considered the consequences of the act, since at that moment the future did not exist. Jessica, much more than Jack, realized the peril her father's enmity presented, and it drove her to embrace what she could have now, before Portman moved to take it away.

Jack pulled the nightdress over her head and tossed it onto the floor, gazing down at her, as slim and white as a china figurine against the backdrop of the patterned spread.

"You're so beautiful, Jesse," he murmured, lowering his head to her breasts and seeking them with his mouth. *"Si belle."* His face was flushed, his skin on fire, searing her as he caressed her eagerly. He luxuriated in her lovely body, desired and withheld from the moment he met her. When he rose to take off his clothes she followed him with her eyes, reaching for him as he joined her and moaning as she felt the weight of a man for the first time.

He entered her inexpertly, almost roughly, and she cried out, causing him to clamp his hand over her mouth. Above his fingers her frightened gaze sought his, and he silently cursed his limited experience. A few frantic nights spent in the backseat of his car with some local girls of questionable virtue had not prepared him to handle this.

"It's all right," he whispered, pulling her closer and covering her face with kisses. "It always hurts a little the first time. Just relax and it will get better."

Jessica relaxed, and it got better. By the end she was clutching him, lost in the experience, and they fell asleep together afterward, curled up like puppies.

Jack woke first, in the thin light of a late autumn dawn. When he realized where he was, he shot off the bed, startling Jessica awake. She stared at him in confusion as he wrestled into his clothes.

"Time is it?" she muttered, stretching lazily. She felt wonderful.

"It's six o'clock," he replied, jamming his left leg into his jeans, "and if your father wakes up and finds me here you're going to be exiled to Siberia. When does he go to work?"

Jessica struggled to a sitting position, pulling her robe from the foot of the bed and clutching it to her breasts. As

her mind cleared she came rapidly to the conclusion Jack
had already reached. He had to leave immediately.

"He usually has breakfast around seven-thirty," she
answered, admiring the view as Jack turned to snatch up
the rest of his clothes. She hadn't seen him clearly the night
before in the faint glow from her table lamp. As she had
always suspected, he was gorgeous.

"Are you okay?" he asked anxiously, thrusting his arms
into his shirt and jacket at the same time. "You're not
sorry or anything?"

She smiled at him, and it was a mature, satisfied woman's smile. "I'm not sorry or anything," she assured him.
"I love you."

He seized her face between his hands and kissed her
swiftly on the mouth. "I love you too. Now will you get me
the hell out of here?"

Jessica got up and slipped into her robe. She held her
finger to her lips and opened the door to the hall. All was
silent.

She gestured for him to follow her and they descended
to the first floor like wraiths, not pausing until they were
in the kitchen.

"Will they miss you at home?" Jessica asked, as Jack
opened the side door to admit a blast of arctic air.

He shook his head. "Mom won't get back for another
hour, and the old man shouldn't wake up until the afternoon. I'll just take a shower and change for school. Meet
me in the gym after the last bell, okay?"

Jessica nodded, wrapping her arms around her torso and
shivering as he stepped out onto the porch.

"Are you sure you're all right?" he asked again, glancing back at her.

"I'm fine. Get going. You'll have to run to make the
bus."

He grinned. "It will keep me warm." He still stared at her, and she shoved him in the direction of the sidewalk. Taking the hint, he jogged off into the rising sun, and Jessica went back inside, smiling to herself.

That morning was the last perfect happiness she was to know for a long time.

For the next two months, Jack and Jessica met at Maddy's house whenever her parents were gone. With the inherent cunning of secret lovers, they managed to get together at unlikely times and places, but the relative security of their previous relationship was gone. They were never alone for very long, snatching minutes here and there, but they planned incessantly for the day when the situation would change and they could admit their love openly. That thought kept them going, and with the natural optimism of the very young, they really believed that things would work out because they had to, because they must.

It was January before Jessica realized that she was pregnant. She had been feeling nauseous and dizzy, and in her innocence went to see her family doctor, thinking she had the flu. The man took one look at her and knew the truth.

"But we only did it once," she murmured dazedly when the doctor told her the news.

"That's all it takes," the doctor replied grimly.

Overwhelmed by the enormity of it, she begged him to keep the news confidential. On the way home Jessica formulated one desperate plan after another, discarding them as fast as they took shape in her mind. She could not tell Jack; she had known that immediately. He would want to get married, and she couldn't see his future go down the drain because of her. He had his choice of several football scholarships for college in September, and this development would ruin all his plans. She wouldn't see him saddled with a wife and a child when he was the only member of his family who stood a chance of escaping the mill and its life of poverty and emotional sterility. She would handle this alone, because she knew in her heart that when it came right down to it her father could not intimidate Jack. He had gone along with Jessica, holding back from a confrontation for her sake and that of his family, but in this instance he would take her father on, and he would lose. They would both lose. Jessica could not afford to let that happen.

She was up in her room when her father came home from work that day. When he stopped at the foot of the stairs and called her, she could tell from his voice that he knew. Inwardly shaking, but outwardly calm, she went down to talk to him.

He was waiting for her in the living room, mixing himself a drink at the oak bar. He greeted her with, "I had an interesting phone call from Dr. Carstairs at the office today."

His tone was the deceptively even one he used when he was about to lop someone's head off. "I pleaded with him not to tell you," Jessica replied resignedly.

"The man is a licensed physician," Portman said. "You're a minor. He knows I'm responsible for you even if you don't. I suppose it's not necessary to ask who the father is."

Jessica said nothing.

Portman took a large swallow of his drink and went on. "I've had all afternoon to think about this. Marriage to that lowlife teenaged lothario is out of the question, and so is abortion. The baby will still be my grandchild. I've contacted Arthur Remington in New York. He's agreed to marry you and give the child a name. You'll go to stay with him until it's born, and then you can arrange a divorce. The Remingtons are an old, distinguished family, and you should be very grateful that Arthur is willing to do this for me."

Jessica stared at her father in horror, too stunned to speak. Arthur Remington was the son of one of her father's business acquaintances, in his mid-twenties, a bespectacled MBA who wore polo shirts and wing-tipped shoes. She didn't want to think about what her father must have promised Arthur in order to get him to cooperate: the Portman mill payroll account for eternity, probably. The Remingtons had status. What they didn't have was money. As shocked as Jessica was, she was still impressed by the Machiavellian turn of her father's mind. In one stroke, he had got his pregnant daughter a blueblood husband and himself a Remington under this thumb. He never missed an opportunity to turn adversity to his own advantage.

"I will not marry Arthur Remington," Jessica said in a strong voice, once she recovered it.

"Oh, yes, you will," her father answered softly. "Unless you want that guttersnipe boyfriend of yours charged with statutory rape."

"Rape," Jessica whispered, shocked, barely able to frame the word.

"Statutory rape," her father repeated with satisfaction, pleased at his complete mastery of the situation. "The Chabrol boy is over eighteen, you are not. In this state the penalty is a prison term—quite a long one, I understand."

"You wouldn't do that," Jessica said, swallowing hard, feeling suddenly ill. "Even you wouldn't do such a thing."

"Try me," her father said equably. "Now do I call Arthur and tell him to make the arrangements and expect

you tomorrow, or do I call the district attorney's office? I
know Cal Williams, the DA, personally. That Chabrol
whelp will wind up in a cell at Walpole, I can guarantee it."

"Why?" Jessica said hopelessly. "Why do you hate me
so much?"

For the first time George Portman showed a softening
of expression. "I don't hate you, Jessica. I'm doing this
for your own good, and in the future you will realize that
I was right. I don't expect you to thank me now, but
someday you will."

"Never," she murmured. "Never."

He waited and saw the exact moment when she made up
her mind. "If I do this, you won't hurt Jack or his family?" she asked, eyeing him levelly.

Portman's mouth hardened. "That kid will get what he
deserves eventually."

"Promise me," Jessica said. "Promise, or I don't go."

"You have my word on it," Portman said grudgingly.
Then, almost to himself, "Let him try to latch on to
someone else's money by seducing their daughter. He
won't get mine."

"If I find out you've done anything to him I'll come
back and take out an ad in the paper telling the whole story
to the world," Jessica said fiercely, knowing this was the
direst threat she could utter. Portman's reputation was
everything to him. It was the main reason he was shipping
her off to Arthur's waiting arms.

"This is no time to blackmail me, young lady," Portman replied. "You're hardly in a position to bargain."

"I mean it. You leave Jack alone."

"I think you had better go upstairs and pack," Portman said mildly, ignoring her last statement. "I'll get
Arthur on the phone and tell him to meet your plane. I've
already checked the schedule, and there's a flight out of

Bradley at one tomorrow. I'll have to inquire about your finishing high school. I'm sure there's a night course or something that can be arranged.''

"You've thought of everything, haven't you?" Jessica asked bitterly.

"I try to be thorough." Jessica moved toward the hall, and he called after her. "And Jessica, I wouldn't try to contact that boy in any way. Just a warning."

"He'll try to find out what happened to me," she replied, sickened at the thought of Jack's bewilderment, his desperation at her disappearance.

"You leave him to me," Portman said.

"What will you tell him?" she asked anxiously.

"Something that will shut him up and keep him from running after you. That's my affair. You go and get your things together."

Jessica heard him on the phone as she climbed the stairs, feeling as if her whole world were collapsing around her. It was all too sudden, too awful to absorb. But there was one thing that made her absolutely determined to go through with her father's plan: it was the only way to save Jack.

When the plane left Springfield the next afternoon, she would be on it.

"Jessica?"

Her sister's voice floated up the stairs, ending her reverie.

"Jessica, are you up there?" Jean called.

"Yes, I'll be right down," Jessica answered, coming back to the present with a jolt. Jean must be home from school on her lunch hour.

Jessica stood and smoothed her skirt, wiping away the tears her painful reminiscence had brought. She glanced in the mirror as she walked to the landing, thinking that the past was a closed book, and there was enough for her to deal with in the present to keep her occupied. She must not indulge herself that way again.

She adopted a cheerful demeanor and descended the stairs to meet her sister.

Three

Jean was standing at the foot of the stairs and rushed to embrace her sister as Jessica reached the hall.

"It's so good to see you," the younger girl said happily. "I spotted the car outside so I knew you were home. When did you get in?"

"Early this morning. I went to the hospital first and then to see Ransom."

"How is Dad?" Jean asked, her voice concerned, her blue eyes large and full of doubt. The nine-and-a-half-year gap in their ages had given Jean a different picture of their father. She thought of him as old and sickly, struggling to maintain a failing business. She had no memory of the tyrant Portman had been when Jessica was Jean's age.

"The same," Jessica replied. "You know doctors, they won't tell me anything."

"Can I visit him yet?" Jean asked.

Jessica shook her head. "He's still in intensive care."

"How much damage did the heart attack do?" Jean probed, blinking rapidly.

Jessica put an arm around her sister's shoulders. "Try not to worry too much. Everything possible is being done for him. We just have to wait." Deliberately changing the subject, Jessica inquired, "How is school?"

Jean shrugged. "School is school. Art class is the only thing that makes it bearable." She tossed her blond hair, several shades darker than Jessica's, over her shoulder. "Mr. Danforth says that if I want to be a painter or a sculptor I have to do well in all my academic subjects too. Don't you think that's silly? I mean, what does the history of the French Revolution have to do with creating a work of art?"

"Mr. Danforth sounds very wise. Isn't he the counselor you wrote me about, the one who's arranging those New York interviews for you?"

Jean nodded eagerly, her disillusionment with social studies forgotten. "He thinks I have a good chance of getting into one of the schools, too." Then her face darkened. "Of course I won't be going anywhere if we don't have the money to pay the tuition." She turned her head to examine Jessica closely. "What happened with the mill, Jessica? Why are we in such trouble?"

Jessica sighed, defeated by the prospect of trying to explain something she barely understood herself. "Competition ruined the business during the past several years. Dad was just squeezed out as a result. That's about all I can make of it. I know it wasn't mismanagement. Dad was always a fanatic for keeping on top of things." She deliberately left Jack out of the picture; Jean didn't have to know those details.

Jean put her hands on her hips and surveyed Jessica critically. "But if what you're saying is true, why is someone trying to take over the mill? Why would anyone want to take on the same kind of problems Dad's been having?''

Why indeed? Jessica thought to herself. Unless that person had a particular score to settle.

"A competing company is looking to expand," Jessica said as casually as possible, pushing open the swinging doors to the kitchen to allow Jean to follow her through them. "The owner is Jack Chabrol. He has a local trucking business."

Jean halted and stared at her. "You mean that ex-football player?"

"Yes."

Jean shook her head. "That's weird. Does he want it for a tax write-off or something?"

No, he wants it to torment me, Jessica mused inwardly. "What do you know about tax write-offs?" she asked Jean teasingly as her sister went to the refrigerator and removed a bottle of milk.

"I took an accounting course last semester," Jean announced importantly, looking around for a glass. "Do you think we'll get to meet him?" she went on, pouring herself a drink. "Chabrol, I mean. Have you ever seen him? He's a doll. Real tall, with great big shoulders and a killer smile. He gave a talk at the school last year. All the girls fell in love with him."

"I saw him this morning," Jessica answered, glad that Jean didn't know anything about her previous involvement with Jack. "I knew him years ago when we were at school together," she added, telling the bare truth without elaborating on it.

"Don't you think he's cute?" Jean asked ingenuously.

"He's very attractive," Jessica replied carefully. "He always was."

"I don't believe he isn't married. You would have thought someone would snag him along the way. After all, he's pretty old, almost thirty, I think, and as rich as Midas. I heard he was engaged once, but broke it off. I can't imagine why he came back here with all his money. I'd go to Malibu and buy a beach house."

Jessica smiled at Jean's teenaged fantasies. "Is that all you're having for lunch? How about a sandwich?"

Jean shook her head. "I'm on a diet. So what do you think of the old place? Does the house look the same?"

"Very much the same," Jessica replied quietly.

"Yeah, Dad would never let me change anything. He keeps all the stuff on ice. The maid comes in once a week and dusts the furniture like she's cleaning a museum." Jean broke off thoughtfully. "At least she used to. We had to let her go." Her eyes sought Jessica's.

"We'll work it out," Jessica said reassuringly. "It will all be over soon."

Jean dropped her eyes and traced the wet pattern her glass left on the counter. "Maybe you'll get along better with Dad now, too," she murmured.

"Maybe."

Jean looked up. "Jessica, what happened to cause the split between the two of you? He would never talk about it, and I didn't want to upset you by bringing it up. I could tell it was real bad, even thinking about what it might have been used to scare me. I mean, all I know is that you left to get married when I was little, and ever since then you've been living abroad. The only time I saw you was when you brought me over there to visit. You never came here until now. Why?"

"When the time is right I'll tell you," Jessica answered softly.

"Do you promise?"

"I promise," Jessica said, marveling that Jean still believed that such a vow meant something and would be kept. Well, she would keep it.

The telephone rang in the front hall, and Jean said, "Will you get that? I want to change my skirt before I go back to school."

Jessica picked up the phone as Jean sprinted up the staircase to the second floor.

"Hello?" she said absently.

"This is Jack," a masculine voice announced.

Jessica's fingers tightened on the receiver.

"Yes?" she answered, with as much panache as she could muster.

"I'd like to get together to discuss the deal," he said abruptly.

"What's there to discuss? You're taking over the mill and we both know why. Anyway, I thought we were meeting with Ransom again on Friday...."

He cut her short. "Without Ransom. Tonight."

Jessica knew she should refuse, but the desire to be with him again was very strong. "I don't know that we can settle anything," she hedged. "We really need the final information Ransom was talking about before we can reach an agreement."

"Afraid to see me without that old lion to protect you?" Jack asked softly, and she heard the unmistakable note of challenge in his voice.

"What time will you pick me up?" she said crisply, and she thought his tone was tinged with grudging amusement when he replied.

"At seven-thirty. Dress for dinner."

Before she could say anything further, the line went dead. She stood looking at the framed picture of her mother on the piecrust table, aware that she had risen to Jack's bait.

Surely this would be a mistake. She already knew that the only way to handle the situation was from a "strictly business" standpoint. Yet on the first day she was accepting an invitation that was anything but. She replaced the receiver quietly and shook her head at her own foolishness. It was no use. Jack's lure had always been too powerful for her to resist.

Jean bounded down the stairs, asking, "Who was that on the phone?"

"Mr. Chabrol. I'm going out with him tonight."

Jean's mouth fell open. "You mean he asked you for a date?"

"I wouldn't call it that. He wants to discuss the plans for the sale."

"Like hell," Jean said firmly. "He could do that in Mr. Ransom's office. What are you going to wear?"

"I don't know. I didn't bring much with me."

"Jessica, what is the matter with you? This guy is the town's most eligible bachelor, not that we have many. You have to make the most of this opportunity. Go out and buy something slinky if you don't have anything."

"I'll wear this," Jessica said, pointing to her dress.

"He already saw that this morning," Jean replied, exasperated. "And it's as dull as dishwater. Pick out something jazzy, something with zip."

"I think a sequined cocktail dress is out, Jean. He's probably taking me to Joe's Diner."

"Not him," Jean said with conviction. "He goes in style."

"Oh? How do you know?"

"He drives a Maserati and lives in that new high-rise complex near the falls. Joe's Diner doesn't exactly fit that scenario."

"You seem to know a lot about him."

"He's the only interesting person around here," Jean replied airily, picking up a stack of books. "I prefer keeping tabs on him to watching the paint peel."

"Is he dating anyone?" Jessica asked, and then could have bitten her tongue off as a grin spread across Jean's face.

"So you *are* interested," she said triumphantly. "I knew it!"

"I merely asked a question," Jessica said mildly, and Jean chuckled.

"You can't fool me," she sang.

"You probably don't know if he is," Jessica said quickly, trying to extricate herself.

"As a matter of fact, I do. I know at least one person that he was seeing. I saw a picture of them together in the newspaper."

Jessica waited, and Jean began to study her nails with deep concentration. After several seconds she looked up, her expression the epitome of innocence.

"Oh, do you want me to tell you who it is?" she asked, batting her lashes.

"If you don't mind," Jessica replied in a tone of extreme forbearance.

"Daphne Lewis. Her father owns Lewis Plumbing and Heating. You must know her."

Jessica certainly did. Daphne was a petite brunette firebrand, the same age as Jack. Jessica had known her in school.

"I'm surprised she isn't married," Jessica said softly, thinking out loud.

"Oh, she was. Several times. But she's between engagements at the moment and has been making the rounds with Chabrol."

"You're a fountain of information," Jessica said dryly.

"I try," Jean replied, flicking imaginary dust off her lapel, and then glanced at her watch.

"Oh, gosh, I have to run. I'll be late. I'll see you back here this afternoon, okay? And take my advice. Go get something nice to wear. Don't be a schlump, all right?"

She bolted out the door. Jessica, not wanting to be a schlump, decided to drive over to the mall in Arlington and shop for a new outfit. By the time she returned with her purchase, a violet silk shirtwaist that had cost too much but looked it, Jean had already come home and gone out again. Jessica found a note explaining that Jean was visiting a friend and telling her that a Madeline Giotti had called and would call again.

Jessica smiled slightly as she opened her package and hung the dress on a hanger. Maddy. How on earth had she found out that Jessica was back in town? She was married now, with a little boy, and lived in Greenfield, a suburb about twenty miles from Bright River. Jessica was looking forward to seeing her again.

The receipt was at the bottom of the bag, and Jessica stuck it in her purse without looking at it, hoping that the next time she saw it the figure would change. There was no way to justify the extravagance. She simply wanted to look good for Jack, and that was that.

The horror of the morning had receded, and she was determined now to mend her fences, to get on good terms with him again. She understood his motive for taking over the mill, but certainly she could make him see the light, deal with the situation in a mature, rational manner. They were both older now, adults with careers and a wealth of experience acquired since their abrupt parting. It had been a shock to see Jack unexpectedly and to relive the unhappy past, but she was recovering. She had to salvage their relationship in order to make the deal go smoothly, and she was determined to do it.

Her mood of optimism persisted as she got ready for Jack's arrival. She called the hospital to check on her father and then showered in the blue-tiled bathroom on the second floor. It seemed strange to dress and make up where she had prepared for her teenaged dates, worrying over hairstyles and breakouts, scattering an array of cosmetics and lotions on the vanity tray. The face staring back at her now was older, thinner, shorn of the innocence that had once graced it. She was pretty still, as Jack had said, but different in a way that defied description. She only knew she felt the difference, and carried it with her like a weight.

Jean returned a few minutes before Jack's arrival and stationed herself in the entry hall. Jessica wanted to barricade her in her bedroom, but a request along those lines would have made Jean more suspicious than ever, so Jessica tolerated her pacing and peering through the curtains. They heard the low hum of a sports car simultaneously, and Jean pointed to the mantel clock, visible through the doorway to the living room.

"Right on time," she whispered, and Jessica shot her a look.

When the bell rang Jean yanked open the door and greeted the new arrival effusively.

"How do you do? I'm Jean Portman, Jessica's sister," she said, beaming, and then her smile faded as Jack looked past her at Jessica, who was standing behind her.

One glance at his expression and Jessica knew that her high hopes for mutual understanding had been in vain. He nodded stiffly at Jean, saying, "Hello," and then stepped

around her to confront Jessica, who had to restrain herself from shrinking visibly at his approach.

Jean, baffled, looked at both of them and decided
quickly that retreat was in order. "Well, I'll say good-
night. I have some homework to do. See you later, Jessica." She fled to the back of the house, doing an accurate impression of a shooed squirrel.

Jessica felt like joining her. She had several unformed,
fleeting ideas about pleading a headache or some other
infirmity, but decided to face Jack down, trying not to
consider what delights the rest of the evening might bring.
This was only the beginning, and he already looked like a
thundercloud about to burst.

"I'm ready," she said unnecessarily, as she was wearing her coat and clutching her purse.

"You look lovely," he said flatly, and it didn't sound
like a compliment.

He was impeccably dressed, as he had been that morning. Tonight the suit was beige, with a cream shirt and
brown silk club tie. He had a topcoat over his arm.

"Where are we going?" Jessica asked nervously.

"Mario's," he replied shortly.

"Is that place still in business?" A decade earlier it had
been the most expensive restaurant in town.

"I had lunch there yesterday. As far as I know it didn't
burn down last night," he answered.

Jessica glanced at him sharply. "I was just trying to
make conversation," she said.

"It's not necessary to humor me," he stated, meeting
her eyes.

Jessica planted her feet. "Look, maybe this wasn't such
a good idea. Why don't we wait for Friday, as I originally
suggested?"

"I can disgrace your father, or not," he said quietly. "The choice is up to you."

Jessica stared back at him, speechless.

"I can arrange a sheriff's sale of the house and furnishings, publish a bankruptcy notice in the papers, make sure everyone knows exactly what happened to the mill and who caused it," he went on in the same flat, explanatory tone. "Or I can handle it differently. Your behavior will determine the decision I make."

So there it was. She either went along with this, allowed him to play with her, toy with her like a cat with a ball of yarn, or he would make sure her father wound up publicly humiliated as well as penniless. Jack knew how much Portman's good name meant to him. His status in the town was more precious to him than his money, and he had always liked his money quite a lot.

"I'll go with you," she whispered past the lump in her throat.

"Fine. Then I think I'd like a drink before we leave. Scotch, if you have it." He walked ahead of her into the living room, and she had no choice but to follow.

He dropped his coat on a chair as she went to the bar.

"Water?" she asked, as he looked around the room at the pictures, the family photographs her mother had framed and hung.

"Just rocks," he replied.

Her fingers trembled as she fixed the drink, but she made sure they were steady before she handed it to him. Then she watched as he prowled like a powerful leashed animal, picking up objects and putting them down again, touching pieces of china and crystal as if they were living things. The subdued lighting glinted off his glossy dark hair and cast shadows along his cheekbones, making them seem more prominent. If anything, he was better looking than when she had last seen him, and Jessica felt her stomach muscles tighten.

"This room smells of money," he finally said, turning his head to look at her. He took a large swallow of his drink.

"These things were all inherited. They may wind up on the block very shortly."

"What a shame," he murmured, and she couldn't tell if he was being sarcastic or not.

"I think it is."

"Some of this stuff is old. Looks like your father hung on to everything," Jack observed softly.

"So far," Jessica said pointedly.

"Just being back here makes me feel eighteen again," he said quietly. "And poor."

"Then why did you want to come back?" Jessica asked, bewildered.

"I guess to reassure myself that it wasn't true any longer," he answered, fingering a silver sconce on the wall. "You left me because I didn't have any of this. Now I do, and you're the one on the outside looking in." He drank again and drained his glass.

It was a moment before Jessica found her voice. "Is it that important to hurt me?" she asked in a husky, unsteady voice.

His eyes flashed, and she saw the fires he kept so closely banked blaze brightly for a second. "You hurt me," he replied simply.

"And that's where we stand. An eye for an eye."

He smiled slightly, enigmatically, and didn't answer.

"I wish we could both let the past go," Jessica said miserably, looking away from his pitiless, perfect features. "I wish we didn't have to carry on with this charade."

"You and your daddy are getting exactly what you deserve," he said coldly, "and when it's over you can go back to whatever you've been doing for the past ten years."

"And in the meantime I have to put up with this...treatment."

"Yes, you do, and be grateful that it isn't any worse," he said roughly.

Jessica hesitated, taking a breath. "What if I told you there was a good reason for what I did back then?"

"I know there was a good reason. I didn't have any money, and you met someone who did. That was a good reason. For you. Especially for George Portman."

"What if I told you it was something else?"

He smiled charmingly. "I wouldn't believe you."

Jessica's heart sank. Her father had gotten to him first. And permanently.

"You've changed," Jessica whispered. "You're so dead, so unfeeling."

He nodded bitterly. "I wonder what made me that way." He set his empty glass down and picked up his coat. "Shall we go?"

Vanquished, Jessica shut off the lights and went with him to the door.

Four

Jack's low-slung, deep red convertible was parked in the turnaround in front of the house. A brisk wind fluttered Jessica's hair as he handed her into the passenger seat, then walked around to the other door. She waited tensely for him to join her, wondering if he was really the same person who used to take her on long drives to escape her father, laughing and telling her stories about his large, unpredictable family. But then the car had been his old green Ford, they were young and the world was a different place.

Jack got in, gunned the engine and guided the car into the street without glancing in her direction. Jessica pressed her lips together and decided to try.

"I was just thinking about your parents and Lalage, the kids. How are they?"

Jack pulled up to a stoplight and turned his head. "My father died about five years ago."

"I'm sorry."

He snorted. "It was hardly a surprise. Everyone was amazed he lasted as long as he did. Cirrhosis finally got him."

"And your mother?"

"As soon as I could put the money together I bought her a place in Canada. She's back there now, raising the rest of the brood. She lives near Lalage and her husband and their two little girls."

"So you're the only one left this side of the border."

"Oh, yes. I'm an American now, a citizen. I even talk like a native."

Again, his tone could have been tinged with irony, or maybe she was imagining it. She could hardly take anything he said at face value. "I noticed that. I . . . miss the accent."

The light changed and the car surged forward. "Sometimes, so do I."

Jessica sensed a slight easing of the strained atmosphere and felt bold enough to ask, "Did you like playing professional football?"

He laughed mirthlessly. "It wasn't a question of liking it. Playing football was the only thing people were willing to pay me a lot of money to do. Choice didn't figure into the plan very heavily."

"You used to enjoy football in school," Jessica said.

"I enjoyed winning games and getting a break from people in the town who would have spit on me otherwise. Besides, comparing high school football with the pro game is like comparing a pistol shot with a cannon blast."

"So you quit?"

"I was fired. My knee fired me."

"Your knee."

"Yeah. I tore it up so many times that finally it just couldn't be repaired anymore. So I decided to take the money and run, invest it in a business."

"That seems to have worked out very well."

"My firm is successful, if that's what you mean." He turned into the parking lot of Mario's, a low brick structure illuminated by floodlights and lanterns strung in the surrounding gardens. A valet took the car, greeting Jack by name, and the maître d' led them to a secluded table sheltered from the rest of the crowd by a wall of standing plants. A blaze roared in a fireplace to their left, and to the right a bay window displayed a view of the turning trees, bathed in a mellow glow from the overhead lamps.

"This is beautiful," Jessica said as they were seated.

"There was a time when I would have given anything to be able to take you to a place like this," Jack replied.

"Is that why we're here? Do you want to prove something to me?"

The wine steward approached and Jack ordered something while Jessica waited. But when the man left it was clear Jack had no intention of answering her question.

"I'm interested in your marriage," he said, leaning forward and folding his arms on his closed menu. "Tell me about it."

"There's nothing to tell," Jessica replied shortly. "It didn't work out."

"Why not?"

"Why does any marriage break up? We weren't suited, that's all."

"That surprises me. According to your father, your husband was perfect for you. Old family, promising career. How could you fail to get along with a paragon like that?"

Jessica looked at him over the expanse of the white linen tablecloth, longing to tell him the truth. But he probably wouldn't believe her, as he'd said. And if he did believe her, he might well carry out his threat to ruin her father publicly. For, while the truth exonerated her, it condemned her father more completely. If she could just endure these lacerating questions, the undertone of derision, she would be able to keep Jack at bay until the the deal was closed.

"I was too young, I think. I didn't know my own mind," she finally said.

"I'd have to agree with that," he commented sarcastically. "Until the day you disappeared you thought you were in love with me." Then he lifted one shoulder. "At least that's what you were saying."

"Jack . . ."

The steward arrived with the wine and poured a glass for each of them. Jack picked his up and drank down a third of it.

"Tell me," he said, replacing the crystal goblet on the snowy damask cloth. "Were you seeing him at the same time you were seeing me? It wasn't a sudden, whirlwind romance, was it? I mean, I've had ten years to think about this. All those weekend trips to visit your aunt in New York. Were they a cover for your relationship with this guy?"

"There was never anyone but you," Jessica whispered. God knew that was true enough.

"Then how the hell did you wind up married to somebody else?" he demanded grimly.

"Jack, do we have to go into all of this now?" Jessica asked faintly.

"Yes, we do," he answered. "I want to know, and you're going to tell me."

"It . . . The circumstances were unusual," Jessica said desperately.

"Oh, I'm sure. Was he a better lover than I was? I know we only had that one time, but I naively believed it meant something to you."

"It did!"

"Did your husband realize you weren't a virgin? Did you tell him about me, about us?" He went on as if she hadn't spoken.

Jessica put her hand over her eyes. "You told me we were coming here to discuss business," she said huskily.

"We'll get to that. I just want to clear away these preliminaries first. You must indulge my curiosity. I've been wondering about all of this for a very long time." He picked up her wineglass and handed it to her. "Have some of your drink. You look a little pale."

Jessica turned her head away from it, and he set the goblet down again.

"How long were you married?" he asked, resuming the inquisition.

"Less than a year," Jessica answered, clearing her throat.

"Ah. Trouble must have entered paradise fairly quickly."

There was no reply to that, and Jessica made none.

"Or was he just dull?" Jack asked. "I mean, you have to admit I was always colorful. Grubby, true, and certainly a far cry from the social register, but interesting in my own exotic, reprobate way."

"Please," Jessica said as the waiter approached them.

Their menus lay untouched on the table. Jack didn't ask Jessica what she wanted, and he didn't ask the waiter to come back. He could see Jessica didn't give a damn. He ordered something for himself and told the waiter that the lady would have the same.

"I'm going to the rest room," Jessica said, rising.

Jack was on his feet immediately. "Running?" he said into her ear as he held her chair.

She stepped past him and found the powder room in a hallway off the reception area. Once inside, she leaned against the wall and closed her eyes, grateful for the silence.

She wondered what to do. Part of her wanted to walk right out the door of the restaurant, and another part wanted to detail her entire personal history to Jack regardless of the consequences. It was easy to say that it would be all over soon, and another to face Jack's stinging sarcasm. She knew that she was responsible for the change in his personality and wished fervently that there was some way to repair the damage that had been done.

After a few minutes she straightened and combed her hair and redid her lipstick. Then she squared her shoulders and returned to the table where Jack was polishing off the bottle of wine.

"Back for round two?" he asked mildly, saluting her with his glass.

"I hope not." She sat and toyed with her napkin as he studied her remote expression.

"Then you're going to be disappointed, Jesse."

It was the first time that evening he'd called her by name.

"You always used to run away when you were upset," he went on. "As if you had to hide it."

His reference to their shared past almost undid her. She waited a moment, then said, "My father didn't go in much for displays of emotion. He liked quiet, well-behaved girls. I guess those habits die hard."

"Ransom told me that you have no assets outside the mill," Jack interjected suddenly. "Is that true?"

Jessica nodded. "My father borrowed against the house to try to pay off some of the business debts, and now it has a big mortgage. Jean is going to school in the fall, and tuition is expensive. Not to mention the care my father will require."

"You really are in a fix, aren't you?" Jack said with undisguised satisfaction. "How is the old man, anyway? Dying, I hope?"

Jessica looked away. "That's an awful thing to say."

"Oh, I do beg your pardon. What, may I ask, is his condition?"

"Not good. I don't know what's going to happen with him. I try to be cheerful for Jean's sake, but the doctors all sound very grave when they discuss his case. It isn't encouraging."

"I thought nothing could fell him. He seemed indestructible," Jack said bluntly.

"His problems during the past few years just wore him down," Jessica said. "I don't think this would have happened to him if things had been going well."

"So I am to blame?" Jack asked archly.

"Do you think so?" Jessica countered, unwilling to point the finger at him.

"I hope so."

"You're happy that you've reduced my father to this," Jessica said disgustedly, shaking her head.

"You sound like you still care about him," Jack said.

"Of course I do. He's my father."

"So you've forgiven him for what he tried to do to us?" Jack asked.

What he did do, Jessica corrected him silently. "I feel a duty toward him, a responsibility," Jessica answered thoughtfully. "But I guess that isn't the same thing as love, is it?"

"Don't ask me," Jack said shortly. "I'm hardly an authority on that subject."

The waiter brought their food. Neither seemed much interested in eating it.

"He always hated me," Jack mused after the waiter left, and it was a moment before Jessica realized that he was still talking about her father. She pushed a scallop around on her plate, unable to refute him.

"I saw him a few times, around town, before he got sick," Jack went on. "He always looked right through me. He couldn't acknowledge that I hadn't turned out to be the bum he'd predicted I would be."

"Is that why you came back to Bright River? To show him?" Jessica asked.

"To show all of them," Jack replied. "And I have."

"Are you happy, then?"

He looked at her as if she'd confused him. "Happy?" he echoed. He seemed puzzled by the question.

"You achieved your goals. You must be pleased."

"I didn't achieve all of them," he replied, eyeing her steadily until she was forced to glance away.

He realized that his bottle was empty and signaled the steward.

Jessica covered his hand with hers. "Jack, please don't drink any more."

He withdrew his hand, smiling unpleasantly. "You would deny me my Dutch courage?"

"You don't need it."

"Yes, I do." When the steward approached, Jack ordered another bottle.

Jessica thought he'd had more than enough. Although his speech was unchanged and he seemed completely alert, she knew that the Scotch at her father's house, followed by the wine on an empty stomach, would surely have an effect.

"You might as well eat something," he said. "It's very good."

"How would you know?" Jessica asked, indicating his full plate.

He shrugged. "I've had it before." He poured himself another drink. "Tell me about your job," he said. "Do you like living abroad?"

"Yes, it's fascinating," she replied. "I'm in Italy now, in Florence."

"Do you miss home?"

"Always."

"Bright River is such a hospitable town," he said cynically. "Why didn't you ever come back?"

How did he know that? Had he been waiting for her to show up?

"Travel is expensive," she said lamely. "And my work keeps me very busy."

He let that pass, even though it sounded inadequate to her own ears. At the other end of the dining room, a band that had been assembling for the last fifteen minutes began to play—a slow, sensuous number with a pulsing, underlying drumbeat.

"Would you like to dance?" Jack asked her, and when she shook her head quickly, he said tauntingly, "Coward."

"I don't feel like dancing," she said stiffly.

"Too bad," he replied. He stood and pulled out her chair, extending his hand. It was a challenge. As if moving in a dream she rose and took it, allowing him to lead her onto the floor.

The moment Jack engulfed her, Jessica knew she had made a mistake. The years vanished as if by magic, and Jack's body fit itself to hers in a way that told her he had not forgotten her shape, the contours he had once known so well. The fabric of his suit jacket grazed her cheek as he pressed her closer, and she felt the hard muscles of his thighs flex and relax, guiding her to the music. Her hand rested on the juncture of his shoulder and his neck, and a few strands of his hair brushed her fingers, soft, as black as jet. How unchanged the feeling was after so long. He was still the most desirable man she had ever known, the first she'd wanted with her youthful passion, and the only one she had loved. He even smelled the same, calling up sense memories of that night spent in her bed, when after he left his scent lingered on her pillow, on her skin. His hand moved up her back to her nape, and he encircled it with his fingers, stroking, caressing, until she shivered in his arms.

He tightened his grip. "You're trembling," he murmured to her, his breath warm against the side of her face.

"Jack, don't do this. I feel weak. Take me back to the table."

He forced her head back to compel her to look at him. "I want to make you weak. I want to make you faint and helpless with desire. I want you to remember." His tone was guttural, ruthless.

"I remember," she whispered.

"Do you?" he asked, his eyes glittering in the dim room. They were hardly moving now, locked in an embrace that barely passed for dancing. He dropped his hands to her hips and forced her into him, letting her feel his arousal. She gasped, and he lowered his head to her shoulder, trailing his lips along the bare outline of her collarbone.

"Jack," she moaned. "Let me go."

He ignored her, leading her into a darkened corner, empty of diners, and there swayed to the cadence of the drums, low and insistent. He smoothed her dress over her buttocks and cupped her, almost lifting her off her feet, and a small sound escaped her. She realized it was one of gratification; she wasn't protesting anymore. Suddenly the music stopped, and he released her. She reached out for him unsteadily, in a daze, and he took her hand to show her to her seat.

Once in it, Jessica couldn't look at him. She felt the blush staining her cheeks, and her whole body seemed aflame with it. He had behaved inexcusably, making a spectacle of both of them on the dance floor, but at the end she had been limp and pliant, eager for more.

The waiter came and removed their plates, and she dimly heard Jack asking for coffee. When the man left Jessica finally raised her eyes and found Jack staring at her, his expression unreadable.

"Why did you do that?" she asked him, her voice shaking. "To humiliate me?"

"Do you feel humiliated?"

"Yes, and ashamed. You can't resist the urge to punish me, can you?"

"Why should I resist it?" he demanded angrily.

Her eyes flashed to his face. "Because we're in a public restaurant with an audience," she answered heatedly.

The waiter, who seemed to have a knack for appearing at inopportune moments, arrived with their coffee. They avoided looking at each other while he rattled china and silverware, and it seemed an eternity before he left.

"Would you like some dessert?" Jack asked neutrally, as if the previous exchange had not happened.

Jessica shook her head.

"Ah, you've lost your appetite because I upset you," he said with mock sympathy.

"I wasn't really hungry."

He sighed. "And here I was hoping that my, shall we say, biting comments had had some effect on you. Overestimating my impact on your emotions, as usual. I suppose I should have known better." He raised his glass and downed its contents.

Jessica eyed him levelly, weary of the verbal fencing. "I'm tired. I think I'd like to go home."

Jack summoned the waiter immediately and signed the check. On the way out he gave the stub for their coats to the attendant. When he helped Jessica into hers it seemed that he rested his hands on her shoulders not a fraction of a second longer than necessary, but that may have been her imagination.

Outside the night was cold and clear, spangled with stars. A crescent moon hung in the black velvet sky like a crystal sickle. As they waited for the valet to retrieve Jack's car, he took a deep breath of the invigorating air and said, "This is real football weather. I half expect to suit up tomorrow."

"Do you wish you were still playing?"

He shrugged. "Every time I do my knee kicks up and I remember why I'm not."

"Is it painful?"

He turned to look at her. "No, not usually. I just can't run anymore, and if I exercise it too much it lets me know about it."

"It doesn't seem quite fair. Having such a talent and being unable to use it."

"Life isn't fair," he said abruptly, as his car glided to a stop in front of them. "You taught me that."

So much for opening a line of communication, Jessica thought bleakly. Every time it seemed she might be getting through to him, he brought her up short with his athlete's reflexes. It was like a dance: spin, turn, step away, or a boxing match: punch, counterpunch, dodge. He was always protecting himself. From her? Was she an enemy, and such a formidable one that she required these defenses?

The drive back to the house was silent, heavy with their separate thoughts. Jack pulled up to her front door and sat looking at the facade for several seconds before he said, "When I first came to Bright River I thought the mayor lived here."

"He did," Jessica replied quietly. "In those days my father had more power than any mayor ever elected in this town."

"My mother never got the name straight. She still calls it 'Shiny River.' At least that's what the translation means."

"How charming."

"Or ignorant, depending on your thinking."

"I never felt that way. About her, about any of your family."

"Such egalitarian views," he said derisively. "Actions speak louder than words, Jesse, remember?"

Jessica studied his profile in the yellow light from the porch. "Right," she murmured. "I'm just like my father, and your neat little plan for the mill was meant to humble both of us."

He shifted his weight in the seat, moving toward her, and she could see his fixed, set expression. "I will own what he spent his whole life building, the fruits of all his labors. And he'll be finished."

"Jack, revenge will never bring you what you want," she said sadly.

"How do you know? I don't have what I want now, so I might as well give it a try," he replied, and yanked open his door.

When Jessica went in the house, Jack followed her into the living room. Jean had left the overhead light on, but other than that the house was dark. Jessica unbuttoned her coat and Jack slipped it off her shoulders.

"I'll see you at the meeting with Ransom," he said.

"Yes. Thank you for the lovely dinner."

His brows arched. "Lovely?"

"Well, I'm sure the food was."

"And my company?"

"As you said earlier, Jack, you were never dull," she replied with the barest trace of a smile.

He took a step toward her. Like a soldier reacting to a remembered drill, she closed her eyes. She felt him bend toward her. When his lips touched hers she almost sobbed with the exquisite relief of it, the satisfaction of her subconscious desire.

He kissed her expertly, with none of the rough eagerness of his youth, but she could still recognize him in the caress. He opened her mouth with his tongue, and she slid her fingers into his hair as he drew her closer. The embrace deepened, and then he turned his head, kissing her cheek, her neck, pressing his lips into the hollow of her throat. She yielded, letting her head fall back over his arm, and at that exact moment he released her. She reached out for him with both hands, trance-like. He stunned her by seizing her wrists and holding them up before her face as if she were manacled. His expression was frightening.

"You flatter yourself," he said in a dangerously quiet voice. "Did you think one kiss would make me forget? When this whole town treated me like dirt, ridiculed my family and acted like I wasn't fit company for a dog, you made me think you were different. You comforted me, helped me, said you loved me. And then when Daddy decided that his little princess should marry one of her own kind, you dropped me like a discarded toy and never looked behind you." His grip tightened and she winced. "Did you really believe your allure was so powerful it could wipe all that out of my mind?"

Jessica twisted away from him, her eyes filling. "You're hurting me," she gasped.

"Good," he said, and let her go. "I want you to know how it feels."

He turned for the door and was through it before Jessica had recovered enough to move. She heard his car start up outside as she made her way slowly into the living room. She sank onto the couch, aware that she'd been in a contest of wills—and lost.

Jack drove straight to the bluff above the river and parked his car on the lookout level. For a quarter you could view the town below through a telescope. It made the mill and the houses and the water look as close as your hand. But tonight he was not in a sightseeing mood. He shut off the engine and got out, not bothering to don his overcoat. The sky was clouding over, and the wind had strengthened, whipping his jacket about his waist and flapping his tie. He wrapped his arms around his torso to still his clothes and leaned over the metal balustrade, gazing at the choppy, glimmering surface far below.

All his life Jack had had a horror of duplicating his father's unfortunate fate. He avoided alcohol, except for those occasions when unbearable stress made him grab for a crutch. He had felt that way when Jessica left him and again tonight, when she'd gazed at him across the table with her beautiful, fathomless eyes.

He was handling everything badly, he knew that; in fact, he wasn't handling anything at all, but flailing around like a lanced bull, wounding indiscriminately. He was competent, even gifted, in the other areas of his life, but Jessica was his weak spot. And if she hadn't known that before, she must be in little doubt of it now.

He must not let her get to him. He'd been seduced once by her beauty, her seeming innocence, and it had almost ruined his life. He must be tougher now, stronger. Tonight's weakness, the drinking, the obvious struggle to resist her, could not be repeated. He would be damned if she'd make a fool of him again.

It began to rain, a perfect complement to his feelings, and he turned back to his car, thinking about his hi-tech apartment: glossy, stylish, empty. It would seem even emptier now. After he started the engine he switched on the radio and sighed heavily when he heard the song it was playing. Somehow the coincidence did not surprise him. It had been that kind of an evening. He reached quickly for the knob to change the station, and then some masochistic impulse stayed his hand. He listened intently, staring out the windshield at the pelting rain. The singer's voice rose and fell, the words welling up from an inner source of pain so clear in the sound you could almost touch it. The mournful tone continued until the final line, which Jack knew so well that he sang along with the record softly: "'Jesse, I'm lonely, come home.'"

Then, rubbing his eyes to clear his vision, he downshifted savagely and backed onto the road.

Five

When Jean came downstairs the next morning, she found Jessica curled up on the living room couch, using one of the bolsters as a pillow. When she shook her sister awake, Jessica sat up, glancing around her and then focusing on Jean's face.

"Guess I fell asleep down here," she mumbled.

"You sure did. What happened? Too tired from your big date to make it up the stairs?"

Jessica smiled weakly.

"Well, how did it go?"

"Fine. Mario's is a nice place." She kept her voice light.

"I'm not asking you about Mario's, dummy. How did it go with Chabrol? He didn't seem to be in a cheerful frame of mind when he picked you up."

"He's, uh, moody, I think."

"I gathered that. Very pretty, though. I wish I had his eyelashes. Without mascara mine are invisible."

"You have very nice eyes. I don't know what you're talking about," Jessica said, glancing at the clock. "I should call the hospital. Were you planning to make some coffee?"

Jean grinned. "Was that a hint?"

Jessica was already reaching for the phone. "I would consider it a great favor."

"All right. But when do I hear about last night?"

"Jean, we had dinner and talked about the business. That's it."

"Huh. And tonight at sunset pigs will fly."

"Better watch out, there might be pork in the trees before morning," Jessica replied, and they both laughed. Their Aunt Emilia had taught them both the couplet, taken from a play she'd seen, and it felt good to evoke their shared heritage.

"I'll make the coffee," Jean said, and Jessica dialed the hospital, asking for her father's floor. Of course his doctor was on rounds and not available, and Jessica was looking up the number of his partner when the phone at her elbow rang.

"This is Dr. Schmitt," the voice on the other end announced.

Astonished at his quick response, Jessica was afraid that it did not bode well, and she was right. Her father's blood pressure was spiking again, and they wanted to try a new medication. Schmitt regaled her with a charming list of its possible negative side effects, and then asked permission to use it. Jessica agreed reluctantly and hung up the receiver, feeling irritated and impotent.

"What's wrong?" Jean asked, coming into the room with a tray.

"Oh, Dad is not responding to what they've been giving him and they want to change the medicine. How can I say what to do? They could be throwing dice over there in the doctors' lounge, deciding his fate by chance, for all I know."

Jean poured the coffee and sat next to her sister. "He's not getting any better, is he?"

Jessica smiled, sorry she'd spoken so thoughtlessly. She could see the effect her depression was having on her sister and was anxious to erase it. "He's not really getting any worse, either. They just have to hunt around for a while until they find the thing that works."

"What if nothing works?" Jean asked quietly.

"Something will," Jessica said firmly. "Shouldn't you be getting dressed for school?"

Jean got up, carrying her cup with her. "I have phys ed first thing," she said disgustedly. "Two showers in two hours. On Wednesday I'm always a prune by ten o'clock."

Jessica chuckled and was pouring herself a second cup of coffee when the phone rang again. More good news, she thought resignedly and lifted the receiver.

"Hello."

"Hello, stranger, it's Maddy."

"Maddy! My sister told me you called. It's wonderful to hear from you! How did you know I was back in town?"

"Jason Ransom is our lawyer too, and he remembered we were friends. He told Michael you would be in early this week."

"How is Michael?"

"Busy. Everybody's car breaks down once the cold weather comes." Maddy's husband owned a garage on the outskirts of town.

"And that delightful son of yours?"

"Not so delightful this morning. He's cutting a tooth and raising hell. My mother-in-law is coming over to watch him for a few hours to give me a break. How about lunch?"

"Great," Jessica replied. "I can't wait to catch up on all the news. Where do you want to meet?"

"How about The Terrace Room, on Saxon Street by the bank? The food is good, and it's cheap."

"High praise," Jessica said fervently. "I'll see you at one, okay?"

"Jessica."

"Yes?" Jessica said cautiously. Maddy's tone had changed.

"Jack is back in Bright River too."

Jessica paused, then said, "I know. I've seen him."

"You've seen him?"

"It's his company that's taking over the mill."

There was a stunned silence, and then Maddy said, "Sometimes Ransom carries this client confidentiality thing too far. You think he could at least have told Michael. I'm going to instruct my husband to hide his distributor cap the next time Jason brings his BMW in for servicing."

Jessica laughed. "I just found out about it myself," she said, sobering. "Believe me, I didn't think it was too funny when I heard."

"I'll bet. How about now?"

Jessica sighed. "I've had some time to adjust to the idea, but it's still a shock."

Jessica heard a baby crying loudly in the background. "I'm sorry, I have to go," Maddy said. "If this kid's grandmother doesn't arrive soon I'm putting him up for adoption. See you at one. Bye-bye."

"Goodbye," Jessica echoed, hanging up thoughtfully. She wondered how much to tell Maddy, who still didn't know the whole story. It would be wonderful to unburden herself. She had kept everything inside for so long.

"I'm off," Jean announced from the doorway. "I've got practice after school so I won't be home until about five. What are we having for dinner?"

"How about pizza?"

Jean brightened, then frowned. "I'm supposed to be on a diet."

"An occasional indulgence is good for the soul. Go off it for once. I don't feel like cooking."

"Okeydoke." On the subject of pizza Jean did not require much persuasion. "Jessica, it's great to have you here," she added warmly, and then slammed out the door.

Jessica rose and stretched, thinking that something good had come out of this nightmarish return after all. She and Jean had had separate lives because of their unusual upbringing, and this time together was very welcome. She only wished that other events had caused the reunion.

Unbuttoning her new dress, now fearfully wrinkled from its night on the couch, she went upstairs to take a shower.

The Terrace Room was a sunny café enclosed with floor-to-ceiling glass, paved with terrazzo tile and teeming with green and flowering plants. The atmosphere was so pleasant that Jessica feared it might be reflected in the check, but Maddy had said it was inexpensive. The silk dress extravagance was going to result in a lot of tuna fish sandwiches, and she had to be careful with her funds.

Maddy was already seated when Jessica arrived, and she waved to indicate her presence. The two women hugged happily and then settled comfortably into the cushioned rattan chairs.

"You look fabulous," Maddy enthused. "So thin."

If you had my life lately, you'd be thin too, Jessica thought. "Wasn't this place a warehouse once?" she asked, looking around her. "I seem to remember a tea company or something."

"Yes, it was converted a couple of years ago. I thought it would be easy for you to find."

"I like your short haircut," Jessica said.

"Yeah, well, Mike Jr. decided that he liked to pull on it when it was longer. It was either this or be plucked bald."

"It's very becoming," Jessica said, laughing.

They discussed local events for a while, people they had gone to school with and what they were doing now. Then, after they had ordered, Maddy picked up her water glass, swirled the ice cubes and said, "Okay, out with it. What's this about Jack taking over your father's business?"

Jessica told her what had happened in Ransom's office.

Maddy stared at her. "You're saying that Jack's been buying up shares and at the same time competing with your father, so that when the time came your dad would be unable to fight a takeover."

"That's right."

Maddy shook her head slowly in awe. "Wow," she mumbled, taking it in. Then, "It must have been weird seeing him after so long."

"Weird doesn't quite describe it."

Maddy fidgeted a little more and then said rapidly, "If you don't want to talk about this, just tell me and I'll drop it. But you've never said why you left town so suddenly when we were juniors. I mean, one day you were in school, the next day you were gone, just like that, and your father was telling everybody that you'd gotten *married*, for God's sake. To whom? I knew you were crazy about Jack. It didn't make sense. And then the first thing I knew you were writing me from Europe, no less, telling me you had a job there. I had tried to get your address before that, but your father said he didn't have it.''

"He didn't," Jessica replied quietly. "After I divorced I wouldn't give it to him. I didn't want him to know where I was."

Maddy stared at her. "You mean you really did get married? I thought that was some dodge your father cooked up to get Jack off your trail. He nearly went mad trying to find you in the beginning, and then one day he just...stopped. Wouldn't talk about you or anything."

"That must have been after my father had his little chat with him," Jessica said bitterly.

"I knew it must have been something dreadful, but you never mentioned it in your letters, and when even Jean said she didn't know, I thought it best not to ask."

"That must have been very hard for you," Jessica said, smiling.

Maddy grinned back. "It was, and I think I deserve my reward. Aren't you going to tell me now? The mystery has been killing me for almost ten years."

Jessica hesitated.

"It's all right," Maddy said, eyeing her seriously. "I know I used to have a black belt in gossip, but I've retired it. Even I had to grow up sometime. Hey, come on, you know I'm trustworthy. I never told anyone about you and Jack," she concluded piously.

"That's right, you never did."

"Well?"

"Jack can't know about this," Jessica warned.

"He won't hear it from me. He hardly speaks to me anyway. I think he suspected I was in touch with you back then and wouldn't tell him where you were."

"I'm sorry if he blamed you for any of it."

Maddy waited expectantly.

Jessica began the story and soon the words tumbled over each other in their rush to get out and be heard. Her mouth was dry when she finished the monologue, which Maddy had received in uncharacteristic silence. Jessica had taken a sip of her iced tea before she looked up at Maddy and realized that her friend's dark eyes were filled with tears.

"What a tragedy for you," Maddy whispered. "For both of you. Poor Jack."

"I would never have left him otherwise, Maddy. You have to understand that."

"Of course I understand," Maddy said soothingly. "It makes perfect sense now." She patted Jessica's free hand.

"And to see him after all this time, it's so hard, especially under these circumstances. It's breaking my heart, Madeline."

"Well, you have to tell him," Maddy said, outraged, as if there were no other possible course of action. "You have to tell him the truth right now, all of it, before things get any worse."

Jessica shook her head sadly. "He wouldn't believe me. You don't know him, how bitter, remorseless he's become. He bought my father's story, and we both know how convincing George Portman could be. He warned me he would tell Jack something to make sure he wouldn't follow me, and that's exactly what happened. Jack would think I was making my story up to excuse what I did."

"Then get proof of what really happened! Show it to him."

"How?" Jessica asked despairingly. "Dr. Carstairs is dead, my father can't even talk, and the last thing on earth my ex-husband would do is help me. After I lost the baby he wanted to continue the marriage, and I...refused. The divorce was not amicable. He felt used, as he certainly should have, and I haven't heard a word from him since I moved out of his place. I think if I approached him about this he would slam his door in my face."

"How about hospital records?" Maddy asked logically as the waitress deposited their salads on the table. "They would show the date of the miscarriage, wouldn't they?"

"Jack would say the baby was Arthur's," Jessica answered quietly.

Maddy's eyes widened.

Jessica nodded. "I'm sure my father told him that I was sleeping with Arthur while I was seeing him. Jack hinted as much, and it would be just like my father to play on that insecurity. Jack always felt that he didn't quite measure up, that someone more 'suitable' would be better for me in the long run. My dear daddy told him exactly what he was afraid of, precisely what he would believe."

"Oh, Jessica," Maddy said inadequately. For once in her life, words seemed to be failing her.

Jessica turned her head to look out the window and watched an amber leaf tumble to the ground. "Can you imagine how he felt, believing that after he had been the first, I went on to someone else so quickly, as if what we had together was meaningless?" she said. "He thought I had treated him like some beautiful whore, having my fun with the local talent, but making sure to keep my hand in with the 'proper' choice Daddy would approve." Jessica paused and pressed her lips together, striving for control. "My father knew just what to say," she ended softly.

"What are you going to do now?" Maddy asked, sniffling and fishing in her purse.

"The best I can," Jessica said simply. "I'm meeting with Jack at Ransom's office on Friday to finalize the deal."

Maddy came up with a tissue and blew her nose. "That's one of the saddest stories I've ever heard, and to think it happened to you," Maddy said. "I don't know how you can stand it."

"I suppose you can get used to anything," Jessica replied.

"Maybe what's happening to your father now is a trade-off for the way he interfered in your life," Maddy mused aloud.

"Jack engineered it," Jessica said. "It was his plan from the beginning."

"Maybe he is just the instrument of fate," Maddy said.

"Jack wouldn't like to think so," Jessica replied quietly. "He takes great pride in the success of his clever little scheme."

"Then his turn will come, too," Maddy observed, and Jessica felt a chill.

"Do you think it works like that?" she asked. "We eventually pay, in some fashion, for the wrong we do?"

"I don't know. Sometimes I wish it were true. Your father really messed things up for you, didn't he?"

Jessica nodded silently, her eyes on the beveled glass she held.

"For Jack too," Maddy said. "You have no idea what he was like when you left."

Jessica looked up at her.

"He was devastated, Jessica. He turned wild. I mean, he'd always been difficult, but this was something else. Nobody could figure out what the hell was wrong with him, because they didn't know about you two. I did, but I couldn't help him. He was beyond reach. He cracked up so many cars the cops took away his driver's license. Fist-fights, brawls at games, you name it. Every form of self-destructive behavior in the book. It got so bad eventually they had to kick him off the baseball team. Football season was over by then, or he probably would have lost his scholarship. The grand finale was his dive through a plate-glass window, resulting in twenty stitches and a broken arm.''

"Another fight?'' Jessica asked, sickened.

"What else? Jack was in the hospital for a couple of weeks. Didn't you see those scars on the bridge of his nose, his chin?''

"I thought he got those playing in the pros,'' Jessica said softly.

Maddy shook her head, pursing her lips. "He was a mess when he came back to school, black eyes, wrist cast, gauze bandage on his head, the works. They were worried about the mobility of his hand at first. The people at Notre Dame must have been concerned about their bonus baby's performance that fall. But he came back to play as well as ever.''

Jessica was silent. While all this was happening to Jack, she had been getting married, suffering a miscarriage, getting divorced. Not exactly having a great time herself, but Maddy's description of Jack's torment was appalling.

As if reading her mind, Maddy said, "I never saw anyone in such pain, Jessica. He wouldn't talk to me. In fact he avoided me. I think the memories connected with you were too much for him to bear. They still must be. He's barely civil when he sees me.''

"I never knew he took it so hard,'' Jessica whispered. "I assumed he would be unhappy for a while, but I thought he would get over it, go on to date other girls, you know. He was so handsome.''

"You didn't give him much credit,'' Maddy said reprovingly, remembering her lunch and picking up her fork.

"Did you think he loved you any less than you loved him?"

"I had no choice, Maddy. My father would have prosecuted Jack, I'm sure of it. I couldn't stand by and see him go to jail, could I?"

"Certainly not," Maddy said crisply.

"Oh, God, I hurt him. I hurt him so badly," Jessica whispered.

Maddy couldn't disagree.

"He'll never forgive me."

"Never is a long time. Don't be so sure."

"I am sure. After last night I'm very sure."

Maddy paused with a cherry tomato halfway to her mouth. "Last night?"

"I had dinner with him."

"You didn't tell me that," Maddy said accusingly.

"I'm telling you now."

"Jessica," Maddy inquired cautiously, "are you still in love with him?"

"Of course," Jessica replied. "There was never any question about that."

"I see," Maddy said, looking at the ceiling. "In that case, you're going to need your strength." She tapped the edge of Jessica's plate with her fork. "Eat. You're appealingly thin, but a few more pounds and it's going to be high-fashion time. And those models only look good on magazine covers. In person they look like Famine on horseback."

Jessica picked up a lettuce leaf and nibbled at it.

"Oh, very good," Maddy said sarcastically. "Everyone knows lettuce is such a rich source of calories."

Jessica seized a roll from the wicker basket on the table and took a large bite, chewing energetically.

"That's better," Maddy said with satisfaction. "And we're both going to have cherry cheesecake for dessert. It's fantastic here."

"Whatever you say, Coach," Jessica replied. She worked on the roll dutifully for a few minutes, and then asked, "Maddy, did you know that Jack was dating Daphne Lewis?"

Maddy looked up from her plate and eyed her narrowly. "Who told you that?"

"Jean saw a picture of them in the newspaper."

"Your sister is keeping tabs on Jack?" Maddy asked, fork suspended in midair.

Jessica shifted uncomfortably. "I gather she reads the society column or something, and she noticed the item. She thinks he's . . . interesting."

Maddy nodded. "Well, I can't disagree with her. He'd be interesting anywhere, but in this slow burg he's downright fascinating."

"So it's true?"

Maddy shrugged. "Even if it is, I wouldn't worry about it. Jack could never be serious about Daphne."

"Why not? She's pretty and very friendly. You remember her, don't you?"

"I remember that she was an airhead, and I have reason to believe that she still is."

"What do you mean?"

"Jessica, she's our age and she's been married three times. Doesn't that suggest to you a certain . . . flightiness?"

"Maybe she's had back luck." Jessica, herself the recipient of some major doses of ill fortune, found it difficult to assign blame for a checkered past.

"And bad judgment. I heard she married some guy she'd known only two days because she liked his *car*, for heaven's sake."

"And where did you hear that?"

"Mary Beth Canfield," Maddy replied, grinning.

"Now there's a reliable source," Jessica said.

"Mary Beth's mother goes to church with Daphne's aunt, and she said—"

"Please," Jessica interposed, holding up her hand to stem the flow. "Spare me. I'm sorry I ever brought up the subject."

"You brought it up because you're afraid Jack has something going on with Daphne," Maddy said. "And I'm telling you I'd bet money he doesn't. Nothing of consequence, anyway. Jack has better taste."

"I wish I was as certain about him as you are," Jessica said quietly. "He's changed so much."

"He'd have to have a lobotomy in order to fall for Daphne Lewis," Maddy observed with finality. Then she smiled roguishly. "Remember that Christmas pageant when we got stuck in the row behind her on the choir stand? And she was wearing that awful perfume that was making you sick?"

Jessica groaned. The memory came rushing back at her: the stifling heat of the choral gown, with its heavy folds and starched, tight collar, the press of many bodies grouped together on the rise of the bleachers and the cloying, overwhelming scent of Daphne's jasmine perfume, filling her nostrils and choking off her air. The memory of the dizziness and churning stomach was so vivid she almost felt it again.

"I saw a bottle of the stuff in her locker later," Jessica said dryly. "It was called Winds of Nature. Waves of

Nausea was more like it. The pageant came very close to a surprise performance from me that night.''

Maddy was toying with her spinach leaves. "I just thought of something. You were pregnant then and didn't know it. That's why the smell was bothering you so much.''

Jessica met her eyes, then looked away, realizing that what Maddy said was true. It was the last thing on earth that would have occurred to either one of them at the time. Had they really ever been that young?

"So tell me about your job," Maddy said brightly, shifting lanes with alacrity. "What exactly do you do over there?''

"Well, I represent an Italian leather manufacturer who deals almost exclusively with American retail buyers. They place orders for shoes and handbags and such, and then my company fills the orders and ships the merchandise directly to the States. I'm bilingual, so I'm sort of the go-between, translating for both parties.''

"I guess all the language lessons at those fancy schools finally paid off, huh?''

Jessica nodded. "That's how I got started. When I was divorced I took a job at the New York office of the importer, and when they found out I could speak Italian I got involved in the overseas traffic very fast. One thing led to another, and here I am.''

"It should happen to me," Maddy said, sighing. "The closest I'll ever get to Italy is a travel folder.''

"Want to trade?" Jessica inquired quietly, and Maddy met her gaze, sobered.

"Things are pretty bad, aren't they?" she asked flatly.

Jessica didn't answer.

"Are you on vacation now, or what?" Maddy went on. "When do you have to get back?''

"Officially I'm on a leave of absence, but it can't go on indefinitely. I have a feeling if I don't call soon and say I'm on my way, my position is going to be in jeopardy."

"Well, maybe you'll get some good news Friday," Maddy said hopefully.

"Maybe," Jessica said, unconvinced. It would take a miracle, and she was long past believing in those.

The two women finished lunch and left together, promising to keep in close touch. When Jessica arrived back at the house the phone was ringing, and she rushed to answer it, leaving the door ajar. It was Dr. Schmitt, reporting that the new medication was working and her father's condition had stabilized. He was still semiconscious, but for the first time Schmitt ventured the opinion that he might recover fully in time. Jessica had known this in the back of her mind, but hearing him say it made her finally realize that her father's convalescence would be lengthy. He would probably require close supervision, and she had no way to take care of him.

After she finished talking to the doctor she got up and shut the door, returning to the living room to place a call to a local real-estate agent. She had been delaying listing the house, hoping that something, anything, would happen to make the move unnecessary. The money from the sale would be minimal, but she had to begin somewhere. She sat with the receiver in her hand, wondering which agency to use, when Jean came through the front door. Jessica hung up guiltily, as if she had been about to do something underhanded. Maybe she had. Jean had no idea how really grave the situation was, and perhaps she wasn't doing her sister a favor by misleading her about it, minimizing her fears. The truth, when it came, would be hard.

"I thought you said you had practice after school," Jessica greeted her.

"Miss Aynsley was sick, and her assistant couldn't take over the squad," Jean replied. "They just rescheduled it for later. How's Dad?"

"Good news. The medicine is working and his condition has stabilized."

Jean sighed with relief. "Does that mean he'll be moved to a regular room?"

"The doctor said he would be moved in a few days if he continues to do better."

Jean nodded. "Great. I'm going to get a drink. You want one?" she asked as she headed for the kitchen.

"No, thanks. There's a carton of orange juice in the refrigerator. I picked it up while I was out earlier."

Jessica glanced back at the phone after her sister had left and decided to put the call off one more time. Then she rose and went up to her bedroom to change her clothes.

Friday dawned cloudy and blustery, a precursor of true winter, which was well on its way. Jessica donned a yellow wool dress, the color of lily pollen, and borrowed Jean's dark green duffel coat, as her sister had worn her cheerleading jacket to school. After years in Italy's mild climate, Jessica had no warm outer wear of her own. She got into the rental car with mixed feelings, anxious to hear the final word on the deal, but nervous about seeing Jack again. His behavior on their evening together had warned her of a difficult time to come.

He was waiting for her in Ransom's office, dressed casually this time in tan-colored cords and a thick eggshell-colored turtleneck. He stood up as she came into the room and took her coat as she slipped out of it. Ransom hurried in behind her, greeting both of them absently, carrying two string-tied accordion folders. He opened these, spreading their contents on his desk.

"Now let's see," he muttered to his two companions, who watched him soberly. Neither of them had uttered a word.

"I just have to add up this last column of figures," the lawyer went on as Jessica turned aside, too restless to stand still. Jack followed her with his eyes as Ransom punched numbers on his calculator, pausing to make notes, and then ripped off the slip with the total.

"Now this takes into account the facility itself, with all the machinery, the inventory on hand and the goodwill," Ransom said. He read the figure to Jessica. "And it's a very fair buy-out offer, I might add," he concluded.

"Offer?" Jessica said bitterly. "Do I have any choice about selling?"

"No. Mr. Chabrol now owns fifty-one percent of the stock."

"So let's call it what it is," she stated. "A takeover."

The lawyer glanced nervously at Jack, who was receiving her comments impassively.

"Where do I sign?" Jessica asked. "I want to get this over with now."

Ransom looked at her for a second, then said, "I'll be just a minute." He went out of the room to dictate a letter of intent to his secretary. Jack, still silent, moved next to Jessica, studying her face.

"I suppose you're happy," she said to him. "You have what you want."

"That's right."

"And we'll have nothing. You must be so pleased."

"I am." He put his hands in his pockets and leaned against Ransom's desk, crossing one ankle over the other. "What will you do?"

"Do you care?" she fired back at him.

"Tell me."

His tone was so intent that, without further consideration, she did.

"I'm going to put the house up for sale, but as you know it's in disrepair and heavily mortgaged. Jean wants to go art school next fall. She already has interviews lined up. It's very expensive, but she's so talented. How can I tell her there's no money to finance her education? She has such plans and hopes for the future. I don't want her to be disappointed the way..." She stopped short, aware that she was revealing too much.

"The way you were?" Jack finished softly. "How were you disappointed, Jesse?"

Jessica raised her eyes to meet his, stymied. She looked away.

"What if I were to tell you that there's a way for you to keep the house, get it back into shape and send Jean to school? You can even hang on to a job for your father. When he recovers he can draw a generous salary more than sufficient to cover his needs. What would you say?"

Jessica stared at him as if he'd lost his mind. "How?" she whispered.

"You can marry me."

Six

___

Marry you," Jessica repeated stupidly.

"That's what I said."

"You're offering me a deal?"

"If that's the way you want to look at it." His dark eyes were fixed on her features, but unreadable.

"I'm not sure I understand the terms," she said warily.

"Then let me spell them out for you," he replied, straightening and folding his arms on his chest. She hardly dared to breathe, waiting for what he would say next.

"Right now, you're completely at my mercy. When we sign those papers I will own everything but the house, which is worth almost nothing anyway. You will have no money to live, to provide for your father's recovery, to pay for Jean's education. I can, if I choose, announce an estate liquidation sale in the local press, post signs on your door, and do any number of other unpleasant things to indicate that you are cleaned out, flat broke."

"That's clear enough," Jessica murmured stiffly when he paused.

"On the other hand," he went on equably, "if you marry me, I will conceal the true ownership of the mill and allow everyone to believe that your father is still in control. Only Ransom will know the truth, and he is ethically bound to keep quiet about it. Your father can, as I said, draw a salary and pretend that things are still the same. In fact they will be substantially improved, since my cash outlay will revitalize the business and my competition will be eliminated. I will repair the house, pay your father's expenses and finance Jean's education. No one will know about this transaction. The Portman name will be saved."

"That's blackmail," she whispered, horrified at his bland, matter-of-fact recital.

"Call it what you like."

"You'll ruin my father publicly if I don't go along with this?"

"I guarantee it," he answered flatly. "And leave the three of you paupers."

"What's in it for you?" she asked bluntly.

He smiled slightly.

Jessica's heart sank, and she locked her hands behind her back to still their trembling. For a moment at the beginning she had almost believed that he still wanted her. But all he wanted was revenge—revenge for the pain she had caused him with her desertion. He wanted to keep her with him, night and day, and make her pay for it.

"No," she said clearly, and then more softly, "no."

He didn't seem surprised by her refusal. "Can you afford to turn me down?" he asked in that quiet, even tone that affected her more strongly than shouting.

"I won't let you use me that way," she insisted.

"And what will happen to your father?" he asked reasonably. "I don't understand why you care about him, but apparently you do. And Jean? Forget about sending her to school. Where will she live if you have to sell the house? Would you purchase your pride at such a price?"

"It has nothing to do with pride," Jessica whispered. "You have me cornered, and you want to capitalize on it."

"Correct," he replied, nodding.

"You're sick," she said, outraged at his bloodless manipulation of the situation and her. "This is perverse. Two people should get married because they are in love, not because one wants to victimize the other."

"Ah," he said sarcastically, "you're disappointed in the manner of my proposal. We should be in a rose garden, with you in a white dress and violins playing as we exchange confidences. Is that the way it happened the first time, when you married Mr. Wonderful, Daddy's fair-haired boy? Did he get down on one knee and declare his undying devotion, while chamber music swelled to a crescendo in the background?"

He stopped as the door opened and Ransom came back into the room. Jessica turned to the window, wiping her brimming eyes with the back of her hand.

"I'll just read what I have here and see if it's agreeable to both parties," Ransom started, but Jack interrupted him.

"We may have a change of plans," he said.

Ransom froze and regarded both of them cautiously. "Change?" he said.

"Yes," Jack went on smoothly. "We may be talking about a merger instead of a buy-out."

"Merger?" the lawyer said, confused.

"Yes."

"With what?"

Jack went to him and clapped his hand on the older man's shoulder.

"Jessica and I have been rehashing it," he said.

"I don't understand," Ransom replied. "I thought we had this all worked out to your satisfaction."

"We did, but something new has come up."

"Such as?"

"Look, why don't you put a hold on this until you hear from me?" Jack advised him. "Miss Portman and I have some talking to do. We have to see if she can agree to my terms."

"Can I be of any assistance?" the lawyer asked, looking from one to the other in consternation.

"No, not with this one, Jason, thanks," Jack said firmly.

"Well, then, I have work to attend to in my other conference room. Feel free to stay as long as you like, and let me know what you decide to do."

"Fine," Jack said, and the lawyer left.

Jessica's mind was racing as Jack turned to face her. Her first reaction of revulsion was changing to measured consideration. She began to realize fully what Jack's plan would mean: a way out of this fiscal crisis for her whole family. But at what cost? There was one thing that she knew for certain: she would never tell Jack what had really happened ten years earlier. If Jack knew the truth, that her father had forced her to marry another man while carrying his child, he would not stop short of completely ruining her father financially and emotionally.

"Would it be a real marriage, or in name only?" she asked him, her face growing warm. "I mean, would you want . . ."

"Yes," he said shortly. "I would want."

"Of course," she said softly. "My humiliation wouldn't be complete without that, would it?"

"There's that word again," he said tightly. "There was a time when you didn't think it was so terrible to sleep with me."

"You were a different person then," Jessica said fiercely.

"Yes, very different," he agreed. "I believed you loved me. I hope I'm not such an idiot as to make that mistake again."

"So I guess we understand each other," Jessica murmured.

"I guess we do."

"When?" she asked, already accepting the inevitable in her mind.

"As soon as possible," Jack answered. "We don't want to keep those bills waiting, do we?"

"Do you have to be so crass about it?" she asked, wincing, looking away from him.

"Why not? I don't deceive myself that you would marry me for any reason other than my money," he answered flatly.

Oh, you're wrong, Jessica thought. You're so wrong. "What will I tell everyone?" she said aloud, at a loss.

"Tell them any damn thing you want," he replied. "I don't care."

"Where would we live?" she asked, trying to take it all in at once.

"At my place," he answered. "It's big, and you can arrange to have the work done on your father's house while it's empty."

"What about Jean?"

"Can't she stay with a friend until the house is ready?"

"I suppose so." He seemed to have thought of every-thing; she had a strong suspicion that he had been plan-ning this for a while. He'd just been waiting for her to understand that she was truly backed into a corner, with no alternative but to accept his efficient, emotionless pro-posal.

"Well," he said impatiently, "what's your answer?"

"Have you left me any choice?" she demanded bit-terly, rounding on him and meeting his cold, impersonal gaze.

"You always have a choice," he said. "You can turn me down if my offer offends you so deeply and try to find an-other way out of this."

"There isn't any other way, and you know it."

"Then I take it your answer is yes?" he persisted, turn-ing and gazing at her out of the corner of his eye.

Jessica bent her head deliberately, refusing to look at him. His gestures were so familiar, and yet his personality so alien, that the contrast chilled her, as if his body had become inhabited by another being. "Yes," she whis-pered.

"Good," he said, nodding once, as if she had finally reached a conclusion he had long anticipated. "Why don't you go on out to my car, and I'll tell Ransom what to do. We can go for the license and the blood test right now."

"I have my rental car outside," Jessica said, as if this were a matter of great importance.

"Leave it there. We'll pick it up later," Jack answered, helping her into her coat. It was clear that once she had agreed to his plan, he did not want to waste any time exe-cuting it. He handed her his keys, and she went to the parking lot and unlocked his convertible. She ran the en-gine to warm it up as she waited for him. She knew that Jack had sent her along because he wanted to talk to Ransom alone, give him some kind of explanation for their sudden decision. Jessica could not imagine what he was saying to the lawyer, but she didn't care. She felt as if her fate were out of her hands now, running wild, carrying her with its tide. When she took a moment to consider that marrying Jack had once been her heart's desire she almost started to cry again, but she chided herself about weakness and held the tears back. When he slid into the car beside her she was composed and ready to do whatever he wanted.

"All set," he said briefly, referring to Ransom. "Next stop, city hall. How long do you have to wait for the results of the tests?"

"I don't know, a few days, I think."

"That doesn't sound too bad. Maybe we should go by the hospital and see about getting your father transferred, too. I hear that place out by the lake is good. One of my drivers had his mother there, and he says it's pleasant and the staff is very competent."

Jessica turned her head to look at him. She didn't know whether to thank him or scream at him for forcing her into this ludicrous sham of a marriage. "You mean Pine Manor?" she asked him.

"Yeah, that's the name. They take people like your father directly from the hospital. They have a special floor for postoperative cases."

"How do you know?" she asked suspiciously.

He met her gaze briefly, then looked back at the road. "I checked into it," he said.

Jessica dropped the subject, certain now that he had been maneuvering her into this position since she came back to town. "I'll need some time to explain this to Jean," she said.

"I'll take you back to the house after we've filed the application, and you can tell her then."

"I don't know what to say," Jessica murmured.

"Why not tell her the truth?" he asked.

Jessica stared at him.

"I mean a version of the truth," he clarified. "Tell her that we . . . knew each other when we were younger and when we saw each other again we just decided to get married."

"Jack, she's not a simpleton. She's never going to buy a story like that without clarification."

"Then tell her that your father broke us up, and it took us this long to get back together."

"That makes it sound romantic and happy, instead of the travesty it really is."

He didn't say anything in response, but when she glanced over at him she could see that the little muscles along his jawline were jumping wildly.

"I guess it's better that she believes in the illusion," Jessica murmured. "At least she won't worry about me."

Jack pulled into the municipal building lot, and they went inside to file an application for a marriage license.

That afternoon, while Jack was booking an appointment with the registry office, Jessica told Jean about her forthcoming marriage.

They were having a snack in the kitchen after Jean got home from school when Jessica broached the subject.

"Jean, remember when you asked me what caused the break between Dad and me, and I said I would tell you about it when the time was right?"

Jean turned from the refrigerator, all ears. "I remember."

"Well, sit down. I want to tell you about it because what happened then has to do with a decision I made today that will affect both of us."

Jean sat obediently, her shrimp salad forgotten, her eyes fixed on Jessica's face.

"Dad and I fell out over a boyfriend I had, a boy I loved very much. Dad didn't like him because he was poor and came from a family Dad considered to be beneath us, lower class."

Jean nodded silently. Whatever other illusions she had about their father, even she knew that he was an inveterate snob.

"Dad forbade me to see him," Jessica went on, choosing her words carefully. She was determined to tell Jean the truth without alerting her to the true nature of her present relationship with Jack. "I disobeyed him because I thought he was being arbitrary and unfair, and because I couldn't bear to be separated from the boy I loved. Dad found out about it, and we had a terrible confrontation. That's why I left home when I did," she concluded, biting back the rest of the story, which she didn't want Jean to know.

"I guessed it might be something like that," Jean said softly.

"The boy was Jack Chabrol," Jessica added, waiting for Jean's reaction.

"I *thought* there was something between you two the other night," Jean said triumphantly, her eyes widening.

"Yes, and now he's asked me to marry him," Jessica concluded, getting it over with in a rush.

Jean was dumbfounded for a moment, then sprang out of her seat and embraced Jessica, almost knocking her out of her chair.

"Oh, my God, that's so romantic I could just die," Jean bubbled. "You mean to tell me that you've been separated all this time, and then when he saw you again he up and proposed, just like that?"

"Well, not just like that," Jessica replied, mentally begging forgiveness for the rosy picture she was painting for her sister. "We had to straighten some things out first, but he asked me this morning, and I accepted. I wanted to tell you because I'm going to move into his apartment while we have this house repaired, and you'll need someplace to stay."

"Oh, don't worry about me," Jean said airily, waving her hand dismissively, carried away by the storybook quality of it all. "I can stay at Claire's house. They have seven kids. They'll never even notice I'm there."

"Are you sure?" Jessica asked worriedly. "I think I'd better call Mrs. Fairley and ask her. You really shouldn't stay here, because they'll be repairing the roof and the plumbing and the foundation, things like that, and the heat will be off and the hot water..."

"I told you to forget it," Jean insisted, hugging Jessica again. "You can call Claire's mother if you want, but she won't care." She began dancing around the kitchen, humming under her breath. "We'll have to line up the church, and I want a bridesmaid's gown with one of those lace bibs, you know, and a bouquet of orchids and baby's breath. And a picture hat, like from the twenties, with a satin ribbon down the back."

"Jean, hold it. I hate to spoil your plans, but we're getting married at the registry office next week."

Jeans face fell. "Not in church, with a white gown?"

Jessica shook her head. "I'm sorry, puss, but with Dad's illness we thought it would be best to play it down," she said, glad she had an excuse that Jean could accept.

"Oh, yeah, you're right." Jean sighed. "I guess I forgot."

"But you can stand up for me," Jessica added.

Jean made a sour face. "I'm not old enough to be a legal witness."

"Then I guess Maddy will have to do it. But you can wear a pretty dress and carry my flowers, I promise."

Jean brightened at the prospect. "I saw the one I want in Carter's last week. It's a heavenly blue organza with a scoop neck." Then she stopped short. "But I suppose we can't afford it."

"We can afford whatever you want," Jessica said quietly. "Jack is paying for everything."

Jean grinned. "And he's rich, right? Gorgeous too. Boy, are you ever lucky."

"Very lucky," Jessica repeated, without meeting her sister's eyes.

"Does he have any brothers?" Jean asked suddenly, struck by a new thought.

"He has several," Jessica answered dryly. "But they're all up in Canada with his mother."

"How old?"

"There's one about your age," Jessica replied, smiling.

"Does he look like Jack?"

Jessica's grin escalated into laughter. "I'll get pictures, on my word of honor."

"You do that. Canada's not so far."

"Only a couple of hours on a plane."

Jean clapped excitedly. "Can we go look at the dress today?" she asked.

"We certainly can. Go upstairs and change, and we'll drive over to Carter's before it closes. I'm going to call Claire's mother before we leave."

Jean dashed out of the room and then ran back in again, kissing Jessica rapidly on the cheek. "You are the best sister ever," she said enthusiastically and took off down the hall once more.

It's worth it, Jessica thought as she heard Jean lope up the stairs. It was worth it for Jean to go to school, have a decent place to live and not agonize about their father, who would be cared for until he got well. Jean wouldn't be concerned about her sister, either, because she now believed that Jessica was happy, about to marry the man of her dreams. Jack could make all these things possible with a wave of his magic checkbook, and Jessica would take whatever went along with that, because she had to. She had proved before that in a pinch she could do what was necessary, and she was going to do it now.

She went to call Claire's mother and arrange for Jean to stay at her house.

Jack let himself into his empty office and sank wearily into his swivel chair. It had been a long day. He'd made all the arrangements for the wedding, and the last item on his agenda was to call the contractor who'd done the work on his complex. He wanted to get a bid on repairing the Portman house, and although he wasn't sure his friend would take on such a small job, it was worth a try. He located the folder in a drawer and put in a call to the man's service, pushing back in his chair as he hung up the receiver and closing his eyes.

She had said yes. She was really going to marry him. He remembered the look on her face as he'd presented his "deal," the way it had changed from incredulity, to outrage, to resignation. She was going through with it, all right, but she was far from happy about it. And that was fine. He didn't want her to be happy.

Jack ran his hands through his thick, unruly hair, his cold expression an accurate reflection of his feelings. Everything was falling into place, working out exactly as he'd planned. He would have her—at his mercy, at his beck and call, in his bed. He took a grim satisfaction in all of it, but especially in the last. Because from the first moment he'd seen her in Ransom's office, he'd known that he had to have her.

The telephone at his elbow rang shrilly, and he picked it up himself as his secretary was long gone. It was the contractor, and he reached an agreement to meet the man at the Portman house in the morning, distracted, at least for the moment, from his problems.

Jessica found that Jack was as good as his word. By the day of the wedding work was already under way on the house, arrangements had been made to transfer her father to the nursing home when he was discharged from the hospital. A team of accountants was going over the books at the Portman mill with an eye to cutting costs and reorganizing production to make it more efficient. As she dressed that afternoon, Jessica thought that she couldn't have wished for anything else, except a prospective husband who actually cared for her—but one couldn't have everything.

She had chosen a cream wool suit with a fitted waist and a straight skirt for the ceremony. A florist had earlier delivered a camellia corsage and a bouquet of cascading calla lilies, and she glanced in the mirror at Maddy as she tried to pin the corsage to her lapel.

"Let me do that," her friend said impatiently, coming to stand next to her. "You never were any good with these things. Remember the New Year's dance when you practically impaled yourself on the corsage that Yalie brought you?''

Jessica groaned. ''And I spent the whole night trying to get him interested in Lynn Paterson so I could sneak out and be with Jack,'' Jessica replied. Then they both realized what she had said, the contrast between her feelings on that occasion and this one, and they regarded each other somberly.

''You'll be with him now,'' Maddy said quietly, fastening the flowers to Jessica's jacket and standing back to look at her. ''But are you sure you want to go through with it?'' Maddy, who knew the whole story, was taking a very dim view of the proceedings.

''I have to,'' Jessica said firmly.

Maddy shook her head. ''I can't believe Jack is doing this,'' she said, sighing as Jean entered the bedroom carrying Jessica's overnight bag.

''Doing what?'' Jean asked, examining her reflection in the mirror as Jessica shot Maddy a warning look.

''Oh, rushing your sister into marriage this way,'' Maddy said gaily, laughing. ''It's indecent.''

''The man is in love,'' Jean said airily, patting her hair. In the azure organza dress she looked like a southern belle taking a break from a garden party. ''I think it's wonderful.''

''Jean, would you go downstairs and tell the crew working on the roof that we'll be out of the house tomorrow and they can start on the inside?'' Jessica asked.

''Okay,'' Jean agreed, and as soon as she had left the room Jessica rounded on Maddy fiercely.

''Would you please watch what you say when she's nearby?''

''I'm sorry, I didn't see her coming down the hall.''

"Well, be careful. I don't want her to overhear anything to spoil her illusions about this wedding. She thinks it's wildly romantic, the reunion of two lost souls who've been searching for each other for ten years."

"It should be, you know," Maddy said softly, struck by the irony of the situation. "It really should be."

For just a moment Jessica faltered, her eyes filling. "I do love him so," she whispered. "I just wish he was going into this for different reasons. Maddy, when I think about tonight, I get so shaky...."

"Then don't think about it," Maddy advised crisply. "One thing at a time. Get through the ceremony first."

Jessica nodded, wiping her eyes.

"It will be all right," Maddy added, more gently. "He can't have changed that much."

Jessica didn't answer.

Jean came back into the room, carrying her new coat over her arm. "The car is here," she announced. "And the crew chief says they'll start on the interior staircase tomorrow, if that's all right."

"Whatever Jack told them is fine," Jessica answered vaguely, looking around for her purse. Maddy handed it to her, her expression worried, watchful.

"We'd better go," Jean urged. "You don't want to be late."

Jessica picked up her bag and looked from one to the other, her sister full of anticipation, her friend doing a good job of masking her concern.

"I'm ready," she announced, and the three women descended the stairs to get into the waiting car.

The drive to the registry office was short, and Jack was waiting for them there with his witness, the office manager of his complex. Jack looked disturbingly handsome in a dark gray, three-piece suit with a white carnation in his lapel, but Jessica was too nervous to appreciate it. They stood together on the worn flowered carpet with the chill October sunlight pouring through the long windows of the colonial building, and were married by the town official. He guided them through the mercifully brief ceremony and shook hands with both of them at its end. Jean handed Jessica her bouquet and tossed rice as Maddy looked on, her large dark eyes missing nothing.

Jack had insisted on taking all of the participants out to dinner afterward, for the sake of appearances, and Jessica had been too weary to argue the point. So that evening, as the sun was setting, they left the municipal lot and drove to Mario's. There they met Maddy's husband and the office manager's wife, as well as Jean's date. A small room had been set aside for them, complete with music and a serving staff, and the maître d' hovered nearby, making sure that "Mr. Jack" was pleased with the arrangements. Jessica tried to eat the excellent dinner, but every time she looked up she saw Jack watching her, his expression unfathomable, and her appetite retreated further into hiding.

"Let's dance," he finally said, and before she could demur he had practically carried her to the tiny dance floor. From that vantage point she could see her guests, who appeared to be enjoying themselves immensely, except for Maddy. She was pushing her food around on her plate while her husband carried on an animated conversation with Jack's office manager.

"You'd better try to look happy," Jack said harshly into her ear as he waltzed her past Jean and her partner, who were welded to each other in the current teenaged version of a slow dance.

"Is that a threat?" she replied, too emotionally exhausted to care about the risk of antagonizing him.

"A piece of advice. You don't want to alarm your guests."

Jessica looked up at him, manufacturing a smile, but her eyes didn't change.

"Is that supposed to be an improvement?" he demanded.

"What do you want?" she asked wearily. "For me to be dewy-eyed with happiness, an eager, blushing bride? You forced me to go through with this, but you can't force me to look enthusiastic about it."

"You look like you're on your way to the guillotine," he observed, gazing down at her.

"Am I?" she whispered, her nerve suddenly failing.

"It's been my experience that people generally get what's coming to them," he replied coolly.

"You never give an inch," she murmured, searching his face. "Not even on your wedding day."

"What did you expect?"

"I don't know," she answered, ducking her head so she wouldn't have to look at him. "But feeling about me the way you do..." She let the sentence trail off into nothingness, unable to complete it.

"How do I feel about you?" he asked. If she'd been looking at him she would have noticed the intensity of his expression—his motionless, calculating wait for her answer.

"You hate me," she murmured.

He didn't react for a moment, and then he released her, leading her back to the table and excusing himself quickly. Puzzled, Jessica stared after him and watched him go to the portable bar in the corner and ask for a drink. He downed it in one gulp, and she turned away to face Maddy, who was blocking her path.

"How are you doing?" Maddy asked.

"Okay, I guess," Jessica answered, managing a weak smile.

"Where's the groom?"

Jessica nodded in the direction of the bar.

"Fortifying himself for the big night?" Maddy asked, and Jessica cringed.

"Sorry," Maddy said. "He looks great, though, doesn't he? Damn his eyes."

"Don't say that," Jessica admonished her.

"Okay, I won't say it. Who's that guy with Jean?"

"The president of the student council. Can you believe it? I heard him ask Jack for his autograph."

"He doesn't look old enough to remember Jack's playing days."

"He looks twelve, or maybe I'm just getting senile."

"Don't be silly. Nobody has acne at twelve. Except me. I had it at nine."

Jessica chuckled. "You can always make me laugh."

Maddy put her hand on Jessica's arm. "You'll call me if you need me?"

"Yes, I will."

"Do you promise?"

"I promise."

Maddy sighed. "I feel like your mother."

"I feel like my mother too. I've aged a great deal since I came back to town."

"That's ridiculous. You look beautiful."

"You don't think anyone can tell?"

"What? That you're terrified? Don't worry about it. You're a very good actress."

"That's not what Jack said. He thinks I look like I'm on my way to the guillotine."

"Maybe he knows you have reason to look that way."

"Thanks a lot."

Maddy glanced back at the table and said, "They're serving dessert. We'd better sit down. This thing is going to wrap up soon."

Jessica hardly considered that good news. She felt like the woman in *One Thousand and One Arabian Nights*, who kept telling stories to prolong her life. She wished the dinner could go on forever.

But it didn't. All too soon the guests were saying their goodbyes, as Jean went off with her boyfriend to Claire's house and Maddy left with her husband. Jack went to settle the bill, and she waited anxiously for the valet to retrieve his car from the lot. Jack arrived just as it was pulling up, and he handed her into it, then went around and took the keys from the boy. Jessica stared out the window as he drove through the dark streets toward his apartment complex on the river, her hands knotted in her lap.

"I had the valet drop your bag off at my place while we were at dinner," Jack said, breaking the silence.

"Thank you," Jessica said.

"You didn't bring much."

"No."

"Most women can't stay overnight someplace without a van to carry their clothes."

"I have enough."

"We can stop off and get anything else you need," he said with impersonal courtesy.

"I'm fine."

"Jesse, you're talking to me like I'm your dentist," Jack said tightly.

"I'm sorry," she said.

"Don't apologize," he ground out, slamming his fist into the steering wheel.

Jessica jumped.

He looked over at her and saw her expression. "We'll be there shortly," he said more quietly.

As if that would comfort her. She nodded woodenly.

"Did you give your sister the phone number?" he asked.

She nodded again.

"Any problem with her staying with her friend?"

Jessica shook her head.

"You've decided to solve the problem by not talking at all?" he suggested dryly.

She didn't answer.

Jack sighed heavily and twisted the wheel violently as he turned a corner. He pulled into his reserved parking place and they took the elevator to his fourth-floor apartment. Jessica had never seen it, and she looked around in silence as he turned on lights and locked the door behind them.

The whole apartment, consisting of a kitchen, living room and dining room, with two bedrooms at the back, was done in Swedish modern décor. The clean square lines of the pieces enhanced the effect of the glowing blond wood. The gray carpeting was complemented by gray, green and burgundy striped drapes, and a matching love seat and ottoman in the same fabric were placed next to the brick fireplace. The coffee and accent tables were glass-topped and sparkling, the television and stereo equipment placed in chrome cabinets. The dining room featured an oval hardwood table and six chairs, the seats upholstered in a gray-and-green hunting print. In the kitchen, to her left, the appliances and countertops were off-white, and the floor was covered with pale green tiles. Everything was glossy, immaculate, decidedly masculine, and it took Jessica a minute to realize what was wrong with the place. It didn't look lived in; there were no photographs, no personal mementos, nothing to indicate that a human being made his home there. It resembled an exquisitely decorated, exorbitantly expensive hotel suite.

"The bedroom is beyond that door," Jack indicated, pointing. "You can change in there."

Jessica followed the direction of his hand and found herself in a room that was as unlike the others she had just seen as it could be. The furnishings were of same light oak, and the king-size bed had a spread of the same harmonizing colors as the living room. But there the resemblance ended. The clutter was chaotic: floor-to-ceiling shelves crammed with books and stacks of folded shirts, still with the cleaner's paper band intact, framed family pictures stuck at odd angles among the litter, and piles of towels and sheets, fresh and ready for use. It was as if he lived in this single room and didn't let anything personal spill over into the rest of the apartment, because someone might come in and catch him off guard.

Jessica felt him behind her and turned to see him in the doorway. He groaned when he saw what she was doing, staring at the mess.

"I should have done something about this before you got here," he muttered. "It looks like a Chinese laundry."

"Not at all," Jessica said, smiling. "It's kind of charming, actually. The rest of the apartment doesn't seem like you, at least the way I remember you, but this does."

He looked at her for a moment and then said, "Your memories of me are misleading. I've changed greatly from the gullible boy you recall. You won't find me such an easy target again."

"You don't have to remind me every five minutes," she said quietly, turning away. "I have received that message."

"Good. I wouldn't want to begin this singularly blissful union with any misunderstanding between us."

Jessica whirled to face him, her mouth open, but he was already gone, pulling the door of the bedroom closed behind him. She sank to the edge of the bed, wondering what the next few hours would bring. Then she heard the sound of rushing water outside the door, and realized he was taking a shower in the hall bathroom, leaving the master bath for her use. She was about to unpack her case when the doorbell rang, and aware that Jack couldn't hear it, she went to answer the summons.

A waiter from Mario's, still in uniform, stood in the corridor, holding a silver bucket containing a magnum of iced champagne.

"Mrs. Giotti ordered this for you, to be delivered here," the young man said.

"Oh, I see. Well, thank you. Just put it on the table, please." Maddy was trying, in her own way, to add a touch of normalcy to their unusual situation. But Jessica had an idea that her thoughtfulness would be in vain.

The waiter deposited the bucket on the dining room table and turned to go. Jessica looked around for her purse to get a tip for him, and he said, waving her away, "All taken care of, ma'am. Congratulations, and enjoy it. Good night."

"Good night." Jessica shut the door behind him and leaned against it, thinking. Then she hurried back to the bedroom and bathed quickly, donning a sheer gown and draping her robe carefully across the foot of the bed. That done, she climbed between the sheets and waited for Jack, every fiber of her being listening for his approach.

When he entered the bedroom she actually caught her breath. He was wearing nothing but a bath sheet draped around his waist, and his naked torso was beautiful. It tapered from broad shoulders that were lightly speckled with freckles, to a trim middle, his flat stomach ribbed and corded with muscle. Dark hair fanned outward from a thin line disappearing below the towel to a thatch between his nipples, and it appeared finer than that on his head. His upper arms were well developed, with heavy biceps, and the veins on his forearms were thick and pronounced with long years of physical activity. He had toweled and combed his hair, but it was still damp, slicked back from his forehead, darkened with water. His skin shone in the subdued lighting, and his amber eyes searched hers as he walked toward the bed, his lips parted, his cheeks flushed from the heat of the shower, and perhaps from something else.

Why, he's nervous too, Jessica thought. Then her hands clenched on the top sheet, her heart pounding as he reached for the wall switch with one hand and dropped his towel with the other.

Seven

When he lifted the covers to get in beside her, Jessica could feel the heat radiating from him, almost scorching her. He smelled clean and soapy from his shower, and even in the semidarkness she could see a fresh dusting of powder muting the fading summer tan on his throat. He loomed above her, supporting himself on one arm, big and formidable and thoroughly male. For just a second his expression was open, vulnerable, and she could see in him the boy he had once been. Then he blinked and it was gone. He became once more the adult Jack; professional athlete, business entrepreneur, the semistranger she had married.

Jessica stared up at him, as rigid as wood. When he slipped one arm under her to draw her to him she tried not to resist, but he felt her hesitation. He didn't say anything but began to stroke her back lightly, using long soothing motions that relaxed her until she was clinging to him, her head on his shoulder. It was the first tenderness of any kind that he had shown her, but she knew it had a purpose. He was gentling her so that he could take his pleasure, much as a rider soothes a horse to coax it to carry him. His skin was as smooth as a flat, sea-washed stone, and every time he moved his arms she felt their muscular motion against her sides. Apprehension began to transmute into desire; this was Jack, after all, and she loved him. It was easy to forget their true circumstances as he held her so closely, so protectively, and she desperately wanted to forget them. When he set her easily on her back and began to kiss her with light, feathery touches, she was soon turning her head to seek his mouth with hers.

Jack knew what he was doing. He was an accomplished lover, and he used every ounce of his expertise to bind Jessica to him in the only way he could. There might not be love between them, but she would want him. He would make damn sure of that.

She was growing impatient, trying to kiss him more deeply than he would allow, and he finally held her still, his hands on her shoulders, and opened her lips with his tongue, exploring, tasting. Jessica sighed with satisfaction. Her fingers crept up the strong column of his throat and sank into the shining hair at his nape. He moved closer, his upper body pressing hers, and she slid her arms around his neck.

The gown Jessica wore had a snap at the apex of the deep V neckline, and Jack drew back to open it. The silken material separated almost to her navel. He slipped one hand inside the gap and cupped her breast, his sturdy brown fingers showing dark against her milky skin. She gasped as he found the nipple, teasing it, rasping it with his thumb. She turned her head away from him on the pillow, awash with the exquisite sensation.

Jack pulled her gown aside, bending his head to put his mouth where his hand had been. Jessica moaned, closing her eyes as he sucked lightly, then with increasing pressure, finally using his teeth as she writhed beneath him, pinned by his weight. Overcome, Jack dragged the gown from her shoulders and shoved it down to her waist. He laved one rigid peak with his tongue, then the other, rubbing his cheek over the surface of her flesh as if he could never get enough of its creamy texture. His hands encircled her waist, lifting her off the bed as she held his head against her. His hair was drying into finger-width strands, and Jessica pressed her lips to its sable softness, on fire at his touch.

Talk to me, Jack, she begged silently. Tell me that you remember the first time, the way I do. But he remained mute, letting his actions speak for him, conveying a deep, profound need he would never express in words. He cradled her in the curve of one arm and peeled the gown from her quickly as she hid against his chest, suddenly shy. He caressed her belly, her thighs, until her reserve left her and she shuddered with the sheer pleasure of his large, capable hands upon her body. When he slipped his hand between her legs, she sighed and shifted to accommodate him, pressing into his palm. He gave her what she wanted, and she opened her mouth luxuriously dragging her lips across the surface of his breast. He gasped, letting her slide back to the bed. He rolled onto her, embracing her fully, and Jessica made a sound deep in her throat as she felt him, aroused and ready, his legs tensed and heavy as they imprisoned hers.

He began to kiss her again, but more wildly now, walking the narrow edge of control. Jessica's response was thoughtless, elemental, as basic as breathing. She clutched him to her, running her hands down the spare column of his spine, slick with perspiration. He sank his fingers deep into her hair and crushed her mouth with his as she wrapped her legs around his hips in unmistakable invitation.

But he was not ready to take her yet, though every nerve in his body cried out for him to do so. He knew the allure of the wait, the powerful eroticism of delayed satisfaction. He wanted her needy, begging. She had left him, forgotten him once. She would not do so again. Jack lifted himself off her and she rose with him, reaching out to caress him intimately. He trapped her hands with his and uttered a single, guttural word. "No."

Jessica stopped, startled, the rhythm of their lovemaking altered, broken.

"Don't touch me," he said huskily.

Jessica's hands fell away. She knew why he was holding her at this distance; she might urge him into losing command of the situation, and he would never tolerate that.

He pushed her down flat, almost roughly, and slid his arms around her waist, pressing his flushed face to her abdomen. His skin seared her, and then he drew his tongue from the valley of her navel to the juncture of each thigh, avoiding contact where she most desired it. She thrust upward, whimpering, and he moved lower, slowly, his mouth moist and hot. She was so primed for his first caress that when it came she groaned aloud, arching off the bed. He teased her relentlessly until she was frantic, digging her nails into his shoulders and surging restlessly against him. When he knew that she was on the brink he moved back from her deliberately, and she threw her forearm across her eyes, her whole body quivering with thwarted anticipation.

Jack couldn't wait any longer; his ache was as painful as the one he had created in her, and they could only be assuaged in each other. When he moved over Jessica, she wound herself around him sinuously, desperate for union. This time she would not be disappointed. He lifted her hips and entered her, and Jessica's head fell back, her eyes closing. Her skin was misted with a fine dew, and the scent of her, the feel of her, inflamed him as he thrust and thrust again, claiming what had always been his. She moved her head blindly to kiss him, and when their lips met he tasted the salt of their desire on her mouth. She was beautiful; he would bury himself in her forever. Jessica thought for one fleeting instant that the wait had been worth it to get to this moment, and then she couldn't think anymore, powerless in the grip of the tide that carried them both to completion.

When it was over, she curled against him, snuggling into his arms. But he pulled away, disentangling himself from her grasp, and she felt him get up and leave the bed. Lost in her dreamy lassitude, Jessica fell back on the pillows and waited for his return, his sweat drying on her skin.

It was a long while before she would admit to herself that he was not coming back. At first she thought he had gone to the bathroom or to get a drink, and well past the time when she should have realized that she was kidding herself, she clung to the idea. But when the room grew chill and the faint depression in the sheet where he had lain was no longer visible, she accepted the truth.

Of course. His was the perfect reprisal. He was treating her the way he thought she had treated him, like a prostitute. Hadn't she said the same to Maddy? And you didn't cuddle with a prostitute. You didn't sleep the night with a whore. You satisfied your appetite and you left.

Jessica almost got up and went after him. But she had some measure of pride remaining, and it finally won as she turned over in the vast, empty bed and pulled the crisp linen sheet up to her chin. If he could leave her after what they had just shared, he was colder than even she had suspected. She closed her eyes and, for the first night of many to follow, cried herself to sleep.

In the morning Jessica was awakened by the sound of the bedroom door closing. She had slept fitfully and was alert at once, realizing that Jack had shut the door from the outside.

She got up and slipped on her robe, brushing her hair back from her face with her hands. She emerged to find Jack standing in the kitchen, sipping a cup of coffee, fully dressed.

"Where are you going?" she asked quietly.

"To the office," he replied shortly, avoiding her gaze. He looked as though he hadn't slept much either; there were deep shadows under his eyes, and the skin there looked bruised and tender.

"On Saturday?" she asked.

"I have contract negotiations with my drivers, and we have to make the deadline."

"I see. Let me fix breakfast for you," she said, moving to join him.

"No, thanks," he said, and she stopped. "I'll have something sent in at work. That's what I usually do." He turned to put his cup in the sink and spotted the silver bucket on the dining table. He walked over to inspect it and said to her, "When did this arrive?"

"Last night while you were in the shower. Maddy sent it."

He nodded slowly and then shrugged slightly, as if to say, "what does it matter?" Such gestures were for other people, for happy brides.

She saw that he was picking up a stack of bills from the kitchen counter.

"There's about five hundred here," he said, showing her the money and putting it down again. "I thought you might need groceries or something."

"Five hundred dollars for groceries?" she said, staring at him.

"Well, I figured you would want some other...stuff," he replied, gesturing vaguely. Then, curtly, "I don't want you bothering me at work."

"I have no intention of bothering you," she replied, stung.

"You can keep that rental car for now," he went on, not meeting her eyes. "We'll get something for you as soon as I have the chance. And if the housekeeper calls—her name is Mrs. Jenkins—you can tell her when you want her to come and what you want her to do. I've been leaving her pretty much on her own, but you might have different ideas."

"All right," Jessica murmured. She didn't even know he had a housekeeper. But then he must; the place was well cared for, and he obviously didn't have the time or the inclination to do it himself.

"I'll send a truck over to the house to get the rest of your things whenever you want," he added.

"I have enough to last until Monday."

"What are you doing about your job?" he asked suddenly, and she saw that for the first time that morning he was looking directly at her.

"I told them that I would be resigning my position in Italy. The U.S. manager said that there was always something for me in the Boston office if I wanted it."

"Letting me know you're keeping your hand in?" he asked softly, watching her intently.

"Just answering your question," Jessica replied, turning away.

She heard him move toward the door, and when she realized that he was leaving she spun around to face him, calling out, "When will you be home?"

"I don't know. These things can be settled quickly or drag on forever."

"Can you call me?"

He studied her, his dark eyes looking lighter in the morning sun. "I doubt it," he said flatly and left.

Jessica stood in the middle of the living room, wondering what to do. It had been an unconventional wedding night, and the morning after had left a lot to be desired. But if she thought about it, what it could have been, *should* have been, with Jack, she would start to cry again, and she was heartily sick of her own misery. She decided to do something constructive, and the first order of business was to bring some life and cheerfulness to the sterile surroundings.

She went to the windows on the far wall and pulled open the drapes to flood the room with light. As she turned away she caught sight of the guest bedroom, which she hadn't really examined. She paused in the doorway, taking in the hastily resettled spread on the bed, Jack's cuff links and dress shirt on the brassbound trunk at its foot. He had left her to spend the night alone in this room, surrounded by the perfectly coordinated pictures and lamps. He knew her so well, with the instinctive knowledge that time doesn't alter and circumstance doesn't change. That single act would signal to her the whole tenor of their coming relationship, and she now knew, as Jean would say, what the story was.

Jessica sighed. She had to make the best of it, and she would. She turned her back on the guest room and looked around, examining the possibilities. They were extensive. Jack hadn't done anything to enhance the basic plan, but Jessica had a few ideas. The kitchen had a bay window that she could fill with plants. There was a small enclosed terrace off the dining room, heated and glassed in, like a greenhouse. It was concealed by floor-length drapes when they were drawn across the sliding doors. She opened them and resolved to rearrange the white wicker furnishings and use the little room, as Jack obviously didn't. It could be charming, and she would make it so. They could also use some bookshelves....

Her brain spinning with plans, Jessica took a shower and dressed to go out, concentrating on the things she could change. She couldn't change Jack, but she could adapt to him, and she was about to try.

She spent the day shopping and returned to the apartment around five o'clock. There was no message on Jack's machine, so he hadn't called, and she set about displaying her purchases: fresh flowers for the dining room and terrace, hanging pots of ferns, coleus, and impatiens for the kitchen window, candles for the table. She straightened the rooms and looked around for dishes. There was a set of standard stoneware in the cabinets above the stove, but on impulse she opened the hinged doors at the bottom of the bleached oak hutch. She found several sealed boxes, which proved to contain a set of china with matching long-stemmed glasses, candlesticks and napery. Delighted, Jessica put the items to use, arranging a vase of hothouse carnations in the center of the dining table, and setting two places with Jack's stored finery. As she was walking toward the bedroom to change her clothes, she had an idea and went to the telephone. She dialed Jack's office and waited an eternity for someone to answer it at the other end. She was just about to hang up when a man lifted the receiver and barked into it, "Yeah?"

"Uh, this is...Mrs. Chabrol. I'd like to know when my husband will be finished for the evening."

"Jessica, is that you?" the man said.

Jessica recognized the voice of Jack's office manager and said gratefully, "Yes, it is. I was just wondering when to plan dinner. I haven't heard from Jack all day."

"You mean he didn't call you? I don't know what's wrong with that guy. I'll have to remind him that he's married. We're due to break up around five-forty-five, so you can expect him home by six, I guess."

"Thank you very much," Jessica said, and broke the connection. Any information the office manager had would have come from Jack. He could have called her if he'd wanted to, but he had purposely avoided extending her that courtesy.

For just a moment her resolve faltered. Why was she doing all of this, when he was clearly determined to be unaffected by it? But then she continued her progress across the room, squaring her shoulders. Having pleasant surroundings would make *her* feel better, and that was reason enough to complete her plans.

By five minutes to six everything was ready. The salad was made, ready to be tossed and dressed, the steaks were in the broiler, and the bottle of red wine Jessica has bought was standing in the champagne bucket, on ice. She was glancing in the hall mirror, checking her hair, when Jack walked through the door. He stopped short, taking in the set table, tapers burning in the china holders, the flowers and the plants. He glanced at Jessica, who was wearing a pair of peach lounge pajamas Maddy had given her as a wedding present, her hair on top of her head, tendrils trailing onto her cheeks and neck. He slipped out of his jacket and loosened his tie, coming farther into the apartment, looking around.

"Dinner will be ready in five minutes," Jessica said, walking past him into the kitchen.

He said nothing, seemingly taken aback, as if unable to assimilate what she had done.

"Do you like it?" she asked.

He went to the table and picked up a dinner plate. "Did you buy the dishes today?" he asked, breaking his silence.

Jessica turned to stare at him. "Jack, they were in a box in the dining room hutch. All that stuff was. The willow pattern matches the wallpaper in here, see?"

"Oh, yeah," he said vaguely. "I remember the decorator saying something about dishes."

"It's more than dishes. It's imported Danish porcelain. Did you forget it was there?"

"I guess so. I haven't exactly been doing a lot of entertaining," he replied dryly.

"Sit down and I'll get the salad," Jessica directed.

"I'm not hungry," he announced.

Jessica's steps faltered. "You're not going to eat?"

"No. And I didn't appreciate that call to my office. If I'd wanted you to know when I was coming back I would have told you. This is exactly the sort of scene I was hoping to avoid."

For a moment Jessica hesitated, wondering how to handle his rudeness. Then she made a decision not to let him see that it affected her. She methodically scraped his salad into the disposal and threw out the steaks. Then she blew out the candles and sat down to eat her salad.

He watched her, his arms folded, his expression inscrutable.

"Is that all you're having?" he finally asked.

"Yes."

"You should eat more," he said gruffly. "You're too thin."

"Thank you. It's nice to know you find me so unattractive."

He made a sound of impatience. "I meant only that you could gain some weight."

"Oh, what do you care if I starve to death!" Jessica burst out, throwing down her fork as the telephone rang.

They stared at each other as it continued to ring.

"It may be the shop steward," Jack finally said wearily, turning toward the phone. "He told me that if the men reached a decision he would call me tonight."

"I'll get it," Jessica said, hopping up and beating him to it. It might be Jean or Maddy, and she preferred to handle either one of them herself.

"Hello?" she said, watching Jack.

There was a pause at the other end of the line, and then a woman's voice said, "Hello? Is this Jack Chabrol's number?"

"Yes, it is. Who is this?"

"Daphne Lewis," came the proprietary, almost annoyed response. "Who are you?"

Jessica reflected a moment, and then said, "Hang on, please, I'll get Jack for you."

He looked up at the mention of his name, and Jessica extended the receiver to him. "Daphne Lewis," she said.

His eyes held hers for a long moment, and then he took the phone. Jessica walked into the bedroom and shut the door.

Several minutes later Jack knocked on it. "Come in," she called.

He entered and looked at the bed where she was perched hugging a pillow.

"Why did you leave?" he demanded.

"I wanted to give you some privacy."

He thought that over for a couple of seconds and then said, "Daphne was out of town for several weeks. She didn't know that I had gotten married."

"She must have been surprised to hear it," Jessica answered evenly. "You were seeing her before I came back to Bright River, weren't you?"

"I don't have to explain my past actions to you," he answered coldly.

"I see," Jessica said, getting up.

"No, you don't," he replied. "My life is my own and will remain so."

"Does that mean you plan to continue with Daphne?" Jessica asked neutrally, as if his answer hardly mattered.

"That's none of your business."

"Not part of the deal?"

"That's right."

"So that means I'm free to pursue other interests, as well?" she asked. Of course she had no such intention, but she was striking back at him in kind.

As soon as the words left her mouth she was sorry she'd spoken them. He seized her arm in a bone-crushing grip and said between his teeth, "If I find out that you have even looked at another man I will make both of you sorry you were ever born."

"I'm already sorry," she flung back at him. "Sorry I ever met you, sorry I ever heard your name." It wasn't true, but there was only so much pain she could stand before desiring to inflict some herself. The thought of him with Daphne was like a knife in her side.

His eyes blazed but he released her, and she stumbled backward, out of his reach.

"That makes us even," he said quietly.

"Was she calling to ask you for a date?" Jessica inquired spitefully, unable to stop herself.

To her surprise, he answered her reasonably. "She was calling to tell me about a chamber of commerce thing they're having in December. Some fund-raiser or something, black tie. It's for the museum."

"She invited you to it?"

"I told her I would be going with my wife," Jack answered, confirming her suspicions. "The announcement card will come in the mail, she said."

"Do you really want me to go with you?" she asked.

"Of course," he answered smoothly, as if their previous heated exchange had not taken place. "You're my wife, Jesse," he added, and she clutched the pillow tighter, unable to meet his eyes. She had a sudden vision of Daphne as she had seen her in the news photo, a perfect, curving size twelve. Jessica, who was rapidly dwindling to a size zero, resolved to eat a half-gallon of ice cream for breakfast every day and be voluptuous by the night of the formal.

She looked up and saw that he was studying her. "You should see your face," he said flatly. "Is the idea of going to one lousy dinner with me such a grim prospect?"

"Jack, that's not it." How could she tell him that it wasn't the thought of accompanying him, but the thought of her comparison to fun-loving, carefree, sexy Daphne that caused her apprehension? What man wouldn't prefer her to a thin, beset-with-problems, trying-too-hard-and-failing wife?

"You're going to be there if I have to drag you," he said darkly, walking back into the living room and picking up his jacket. "So get used to the idea."

"I'll go with you, Jack. I never said I wouldn't," Jessica called, hurrying to follow him. He was already at the door.

"Don't do me any favors," he said vehemently, spinning around to confront her. "Do you think I don't know why you don't want to go? All the old guard of the town will be there. They always are at these things, and you'll be on the arm of the spinner's boy, the outcast's son. I could make a million dollars, fly to the moon, run for president, but that's the only way they'll ever think of me. And in their eyes you're still George Portman's daughter. Despite your daddy's best efforts, you married beneath your station after all."

Jessica stared at him, openmouthed, silenced by the staggering unfairness of it, which beggared reply. Such an idea had never entered her mind, but he believed it unconditionally. The scars of those early years were deep and permanent. It was important to him that she show she was with him now, and he thought she was refusing to do it.

"Now I was forgetting the deal, wasn't I?" he asked softly and turned away.

"What are you doing?" she asked, worried. He was wild in these moods, capable of almost anything.

"Isn't it obvious? I'm leaving."

"To go where?"

"To go for a walk," he answered curtly.

"Now?" she said desperately. "Why?"

"I'm supposed to walk two miles a day, for my knee," he answered, with barely disguised impatience.

This was the first she'd heard of such a convenient directive. "I'll come with you," she said hastily, rushing to the closet for her coat.

"No, you won't," he countered, holding up his hand. "I prefer to go alone."

Naturally, Jessica thought dully. Just like he preferred to sleep alone. As she watched, he slung his jacket over his shoulder and left without a parting glance.

Jessica set about cleaning up the remains of the rejected dinner automatically, washing what dishes she'd used and putting everything away. She dumped the rest of her food down the garbage disposal and settled for a cup of coffee, realizing that this was no way to defeat dazzling Daphne, but past the point of caring. She curled up on the sofa to wait.

She had an idea Jack was going to take a very long walk.

Jack left the complex of buildings and set off toward the river, hands in pockets, head down. He was dressed too lightly for the weather, but he just walked faster, warming up with a brisk pace. The moon illuminated his path as he moved along with his heralded, yard gaining stride. His thoughts weren't on the ground he was covering, however, but on the woman he had left behind at the apartment.

Jesse was playing with his head, putting on an act to confuse him. The dinner tonight, the candles, the flowers, the whole scenario had an underlying purpose. She was trying to rob him of his just revenge, because she knew there was no sweetness, no savor, in punishing someone who did not appear to deserve it.

Well, he wouldn't let her get to him again. He had fallen into her trap once, but he was older and wiser now. He knew what she had done, how it had soured him forever on women, on life, on love. All the kindness she affected now could not negate the ten years he had waited for, and plotted, this retribution.

He bent his head against the gathering wind and turned onto the river walk, striding off into the dark.

Jessica was in bed when Jack returned, but not asleep. She heard him come in and try the bedroom door. Then, with no warning but a furious burst of noise, he kicked it in.

Jessica sat bolt upright, more bewildered than scared. Why on earth had he done that?

Jack charged into the room as the door slammed against the wall. He ran to the bed and seized her by the shoulders, dragging her forward and shaking her.

"Don't you ever do that again, do you hear me?" he rasped, his large fingers digging into her bare arms.

"Do what?" she asked, staring up at him.

"Lock the door against me!"

"I didn't lock it!" she protested.

"Don't lie to me!" he raged, flinging her back against the pillows.

"I'm not lying." She was almost weeping, and her unfeigned bewilderment gave him pause. He studied her as she went on, "The door has been sticking. I meant to tell you about it. I just noticed it this morning."

He examined her a moment longer as she pushed back her disordered hair, and then walked to the door, shutting it quietly. When he turned the knob, the door refused to budge.

"Now do you believe me?" Jessica asked softly behind him.

He turned and faced her, his eyes dark with some unnamed emotion.

"I wouldn't lock you out," she added, clutching the sheet to her breasts.

"Because I have my rights?" he asked cynically. He was watching her very closely.

"Yes. Because I plan to live up to my end of the bargain."

He came to the bed and sat on its edge. "How flattering. I'm one of your duties, like the laundry."

"I didn't say that."

"But you think it. You think it every time I touch you." He slipped his hand to the back of her neck, his fingers curving around her nape possessively.

"It would be so much easier for you if I were a man, wouldn't it?" she whispered, reading the amber glint in his slitted eyes.

He almost smiled. "What?"

She nodded slowly. "If I were a man you could punch me, beat me up, pummel me into the ground for the hurt I caused you. That's really what you'd like to do, isn't it?"

"No," he murmured, as if the single word were wrenched from his gut.

"I think it is," she went on quietly. "But since I'm a woman, you've found other, more subtle tortures for me."

As if in response to her words, he withdrew his hand and, rising, turned to go.

She reached up to stop him, her bare arm gleaming in the faint light from the hall. Her fingers closed around his wrist as the blanket fell away from her shoulders, and he saw that she was naked.

Jack dropped to his knees on the floor and pulled her into his arms. He pressed his mouth to her satiny shoulder and then trailed his lips downward, capturing the tip of one breast between them. Jessica tangled her fingers in his hair and held him tightly. When he lifted his head to kiss her, she drew him onto the bed, eager for the only form of closeness he appeared to require from her.

Jack moved his mouth to the pale hollow of her neck, and Jessica's head fell back in abandonment, her hair a sheen of gold on the pillow. He was still fully clothed, but he pressed against her as if he couldn't spare the few sec-

onds it would take to undress, caressing her hungrily. He
pinned her, drawing her knees up and settling into the
cradle of her hips. Her hands traveled up and down his
back, feeling the muscles contract beneath the fine cloth
of his shirt. He lifted himself on one arm and stared down
at her, seeing the heavy-lidded eyes, the parted lips, swollen from his kisses. She was invitation incarnate, her whole
body straining toward him, demanding fulfillment.

Jack trailed his free hand between her breasts, bisecting
her body, over her navel, down to the puff of wheaten hair
between her legs. She watched him, enraptured, her breath
caught in her throat. When he touched her she gasped,
then pressed her lips together, never looking away from
him. She was wet, more than ready, and her grip tightened on him, became almost painful as he caressed her. He
lifted his fingers, moist with her dew, to his lips and
touched them with his tongue.

"Jack," she moaned, pulling at his belt. "Please."

He surged off the bed, tearing at his clothes, tossing
them in a heap on the floor. When he moved over her
again he entered her in almost the same motion, her deep
groan of satisfaction echoing his own. He had no wish for
refinements, and neither did she; they tumbled headlong
to a turbulent conclusion that left them both drained and
panting, drenched with sweat.

They didn't move for several seconds, recovering from
the storm. Then Jessica, stretching like a postprandial cat,
reached up to smooth Jack's damp hair from his brow in
a languid, satiated caress. But he turned his face away,
rolling off her and sitting up on the side of the bed.

"Don't go," she whispered, pulling at his hand, too be-
sotted with him for pretense.

But he shrugged her off and stood, then bent to gather
the pile of his clothes and walked to the door. She put her

hand to her mouth to stifle her sob, but he didn't see her as he left the room.

Jack paused to lean against the door on the other side once he closed it. He turned his head and put his hand up, palm flat against the panel in a gesture of longing. Then, his shoulders slumping with weariness, with defeat, he threw the ball of his clothes onto the sofa and went to the guest room to sleep.

Eight

This pattern continued for almost two months. Jessica tried everything she could think of to pierce the barrier Jack had erected, but he would relent only in bed. And it seemed that any communion they achieved while making love counted for nothing. As soon as it was over he left her, and in the morning he was his usual hostile, withdrawn self. His attitude worked a change in Jessica, too. Usually she wanted to talk out her problems and would press for communication, but with Jack she, too, retreated into silence. She was not going to apologize for something she hadn't done, and she wasn't going to be his doormat. Because she cared so much, her self-respect was on the line, and not even for Jack would she sacrifice it.

So it was that, on a morning in mid-December, she went with Maddy to visit her father in the nursing home, worn out and sick at heart. She had thought that by this time things would be better with Jack, and seeing her father always depressed her. He was improving, but listless and disinterested, a far cry from the man who had ruled the Portman Mill—and her—with a will of iron. Strange to think now that this was the despot who had held her life in the palm of his hand, played with it, and then crushed it like a candy wrapper and tossed it away. He had accepted the news of her marriage with grim resignation, aware that he had lost his power over her life and his fortunes forever. Jessica spoke to the ward nurse about his care, arranged a bunch of flowers in the vase on his nightstand and left. She walked with Maddy to her new car, which was parked outside.

"So how are things at home?" Maddy said as they got into it, making conversation to forget the dismal experience they had just shared. "Any change?"

Jessica shook her head. "Everything is still the same."

Maddy gazed at her as she pulled out into the street. "You two aren't working things out, are you?"

"No."

Maddy sighed. "I can tell that just by looking at you. I had hoped that in time…"

"It will take more than the passage of time to solve our problems."

"Give him a chance."

"That's what I keep telling myself, but I don't really believe it. It's me. I'm the problem, and that's not going to change."

"Exactly what is going on?" Maddy inquired directly.

Jessica bit her lip, then shrugged. "Oh, he does a lot of little things to indicate that my presence in his life has not affected it. He eats out, won't let me cook for him. When he comes home, he says he has already eaten and isn't hungry. He won't let me do anything for him. I pressed his shirt for him the other day and he told me not to do it again, he preferred the way the dry cleaner did them.''

"I've been waiting five years for Michael to say something like that to me.''

"Maddy, I'm serious.''

"Sorry.''

"He's making a concentrated effort to keep me at arm's length. He won't let me get close, and enduring his coldness day in and day out is wearing me down to nothing.''

"What about the sex?'' Maddy asked bluntly.

"It's wonderful,'' Jessica said mournfully.

"You don't sound too happy about it.''

"Jack is a very skilled lover.''

"No surprise there,'' Maddy observed dryly.

"But he withholds himself, even then. He makes love to me and then leaves me alone. He treats me like a... courtesan.'' Jessica swallowed painfully. "I feel more alone now than I did before I married him.''

"I have a mind to go and see him and tell him the truth about what happened ten years ago,'' Maddy said grimly.

Jessica jammed on the brake, and both women shot forward in their seats. "Maddy, promise me you won't,'' Jessica pleaded as the driver behind her leaned on the horn. "It would be the worst possible thing you could do.''

"All right,'' Maddy agreed quickly, glancing through the rear window in alarm. "Don't have an accident. I was just thinking out loud. But I *do* think you should leave him,'' Maddy said fiercely. "Nothing is worth this. I'll bet you haven't had a decent meal or a good night's sleep since you married him. The hell with your father and Jean. If things continue this way you'll be bringing them a sacrifice. Do you think either one of them would want that?''

"It's not just them,'' Jessica whispered. "I love him.''

"In spite of everything?''

"In spite of everything," Jessica repeated.

Maddy sighed. "Well, I guess we'll all be having a jolly old time at the formal tonight. Does Jack know yet that you sent the response card back and said you would both be there?"

"I told him last week."

"What did he think?"

"He *acted* puzzled, confused, as though he couldn't figure out what to make of it. I don't know what he *thinks*. He doesn't talk to me."

"What do you mean he doesn't talk to you?"

"He says things like, 'I paid the light bill,' or 'Have you seen my gray striped tie?' He doesn't communicate. I don't know, maybe it's my fault. I started things off on the wrong foot the day after the wedding."

"What happened?"

"Daphne Lewis called."

"Oh, dear. I gather that was a problem."

"For me," Jessica said unhappily. "I'm afraid I didn't handle it very well." She glanced at Maddy, then back at the road, bending her head in a gesture of resignation. "You don't understand, Maddy. In ten years I couldn't get interested in any other man. I mean, some tried, but it was never any good. Never. It was always Jack. And now, when I see this going down the drain before my eyes, it's . . . hard, that's all."

"I know," Maddy said sympathetically. "I know it's hard." They were driving past the Portman house, and she interjected, "Look at all those trucks in the driveway. They must be making good progress on the renovations."

Jessica nodded. "And the business is turning around, thanks to Jack's infusion of cash. Jean is in New York, touring the art schools, and my father has the best medical attention money can buy."

"Jack's done everything he said he would."

"Except love me," Jessica said sadly. "But then, he never promised that."

"He's emotionally tied to you, Jessica, he has to be," Maddy said. "He would never go to all the trouble he has if he weren't."

"He's tied to me, all right," Jessica answered quietly. "Revenge is a very powerful emotion."

"It can't be just that," Maddy argued.

"It is. Even as a boy, Jack had that unbending, unyielding quality about him. He can't forgive. He won't, because he doesn't want to. It's as simple as that."

"And in your case there's really nothing to forgive," Maddy said softly. "Taking such punishment every day when you know you don't deserve it, I wonder that you don't go mad."

"I wonder if I *am* going mad."

"You're still sane, take my word for it." Maddy turned her head to look out at the frosty December day, flowing past them as Jessica drove. "It's funny, in a way. All the women in town envy you. If they only knew."

"What is there to know? That he treats me like a fiscal responsibility?"

"Nobody sleeps with a fiscal responsibility."

"Jack does."

"Most of my friends would take what you have, be thrilled, and never miss what's missing," Maddy said reasonably.

"But they're not me," Jessica murmured. "I want him to love me."

"You thought you could win him over, didn't you?" Maddy asked sympathetically.

Jessica smiled deprecatingly. "I guess I overestimated my charm."

"Oh, Jessica, don't talk about yourself that way. No one ever had more charm for him than you did. If that's changed, it's because something is dead in him."

"Yes, it is," Jessica agreed, her voice flat and hopeless. "And I killed it."

Maddy didn't know how to reply, and silence filled the car until Jessica dropped her off at her house. The baby-sitter was peering through the curtain as they pulled up to the curb.

"Oh, oh. Looks like it's Ransom of Red Chief time. I wonder what the kid did this morning," Maddy said wearily, opening her door. "Yesterday he turned a bowl of cereal upside down on my mother-in-law's head."

"You'd best get in there."

"Come to think of it, she looked better wearing the cereal," Maddy added, climbing out of the car, and Jessica grinned.

"That's more like it," Maddy said. "I'll see you at eight. You're sure we're at the same table?"

"I requested it."

"Okay." She dropped her voice. "And if you decide at the last minute that you'd rather avoid it, just call me and I'll tell everybody you have the flu."

"Thanks, but I think I'm going to have to face up to this one," Jessica answered, and Maddy nodded, slamming the door. She trotted up the walk to her house, and Jessica drove away, her mind on the dinner that night.

It began to sleet as she crossed town, and the roads became slippery with a fine glaze that shone like glass. Distracted, thinking over her conversation with Maddy, Jessica wasn't paying attention and didn't brake for a stoplight in time. She skidded into the intersection and collided with a car coming out of a side street, slamming into its rear fender.

She jolted to a halt, shaken but unhurt, and got out to see how the other driver was doing. The woman inside the car was conscious but holding her head, where a purpling bruise was already forming above her left eye.

"Are you all right?" Jessica asked as the woman rolled down her window.

"I think so. I just hit my head on the windshield," the other driver replied.

"It was my fault. I skidded when I braked. You should have that checked to make sure it's nothing serious. I'm certain my insurance will cover any damage to your car."

They were still talking as a patrol car pulled up. A policeman got out and took down the necessary information. Jessica needed Jack's insurance card number. She walked to the pay phone on the corner to call his office and get it from the secretary. She told the girl she would be going to the hospital and then followed the police vehicle to the emergency room.

Jessica was waiting in the reception area for the woman to finish up in X ray when Jack burst through the outer door, his hair disheveled, his face white beneath his light winter tan. He rushed up to the admitting desk and grabbed the charge nurse by the arm, demanding, "Jessica Chabrol. Where is she?"

The woman removed her arm from his grasp with an expression of extreme distaste and said frostily, "I beg your pardon?"

"You have a patient here named Jessica Chabrol. She was just admitted—young, pretty, blond. She was in a car accident. What's her condition?"

"Sir, we have no record—"

"Look, lady," Jack interrupted in a dangerous tone, leaning in close to the nurse and stabbing his index finger into her collarbone, "I'm running out of patience with you. Now either you find out where the hell Jesse is or..."

"Jack," Jessica managed to call weakly, finding her voice at last. Her astonishment at his performance had rendered her momentarily speechless. "I'm over here."

He whirled to face her, his eyes widening. "Jesse," he said. "What are you doing standing there?"

"Waiting. Nothing is wrong with me."

He looked bewildered. "The message I got said that you'd been in an accident and were at the emergency room."

"That's right. I came to see that the driver of the car I hit was okay. She's being x-rayed right now."

Jack recovered before her eyes, blinking and squaring his shoulders. "I'm going to kill that girl when I get back to the office," he said grimly.

"It's not her fault, Jack," Jessica responded. "I was a little upset when I called. I probably confused her."

"She was born confused."

"You thought I was hurt?" Jessica asked, trying not to draw any conclusions from his behavior.

"I see that you're not," he answered casually, already regaining his equilibrium. "What happened?"

"I skidded into an intersection and sideswiped a car."

"I see." He looked her over coolly. "You'll be staying here?"

Jessica nodded. "I want to make sure everything is all right."

"Then I assume I'll see you tonight," he said, and turning on his heel, departed as abruptly as he had arrived.

"Did I imagine that?" the charge nurse said to nobody in particular. "Was that nut just here?"

"He was here," Jessica answered thoughtfully, mulling over the scene in her mind. Then the door of the inner room opened and she turned to confront the doctor, putting aside the question of Jack's concern for a later date.

Jack drove back to his office directly from the hospital. The knot that had formed in his stomach at the news of Jesse's accident loosened as he traveled the slick, frosted streets. He couldn't delude himself any longer. He'd been in a panic when he thought she was hurt, and when he'd seen her standing there, whole and uninjured, his relief was tantamount to joy. He was fairly sure he had managed to conceal the depth of his emotion from her, but he wasn't sure he could continue to do so.

The whole thing was not developing the way he had imagined. He'd thought he could keep her at a distance, but every day that passed he wanted her more. And not just in bed. He wanted her tenderness and understanding, her shared jokes and laughter, the warmth he had remembered for ten years the way a freezing man remembers a blazing hearth. It was just no good. He was tumbling over the edge into the same abyss that had consumed him when he was eighteen.

It didn't help to tell himself that he was falling all over again for her tricks. He did that each waking minute and fell just as hard. The knowledge that he had compelled her to marry him rankled, and the awareness that she was taking it all so well, repaying his brutishness with patience and kindness, disturbed him even more.

Occasionally she did flare up at him, but the outbursts never lasted very long, as if she'd forgotten for a moment that she'd resigned herself to the situation, and then remembered again. He felt as if he were abusing her all the time, and he loathed himself for it. His pride would not let him reach out to her, the woman who had spurned him, but his conscience would not let him behave like a boor without troubling him. So he was miserable. Trapped in a prison of his own making, he kept Jesse locked in it with him, both of them lonely and heartsick.

Jack pulled his car into his parking space and went inside to have a little chat with his secretary.

When Jessica got back to the apartment she tossed the pad with the other driver's insurance information onto the kitchen counter. Then she collapsed into the deep chair by the fireplace. It looked as though the woman was fine, but she planned to check again in a few days to make sure.

The housekeeper had paid a visit during Jessica's absence, and everything was put away in its place. The apartment was as neat as a monastic's cell. Mrs. Jenkins was a compulsive tidier and was forever putting items in drawers and closets that Jack preferred left out where he could see them. He complained that she "hid" things on him, but when Jessica suggested that she might be able to take over the housework, he had reacted negatively, saying shortly that Mrs. Jenkins kept the place the way he liked it. This was patently untrue, and at the same time carried the implication that Jessica was incapable of doing so. She realized again that he didn't want her taking care of him, doing the little things that strengthened the bond between two people. As always, he wanted to travel alone.

Jessica went to the bedroom and hung the plastic cleaner's bag she was carrying on the door. It contained Jack's tuxedo, which she had picked up before calling for Maddy, and she realized that Mrs. Jenkins had put away the studs the dress shirt required. Jack always left his few items of jewelry in a wooden tray on the dresser. Despite repeated requests to the contrary, the housekeeper invariably transferred them to a small carved box he kept in the top drawer. In order to avoid another diatribe on the short-comings of Mrs. Jenkins, Jessica went to the drawer to retrieve the studs. She took out the box, which she had never examined, and flipped open the top, rooting around in the mess of cuff links and tie clasps for the elusive polished buttons.

She found all of them and was about to close the box when she saw a thin drawer at the bottom, below the base of the main container. She had never noticed it, and before she thought about it she pulled it open, wondering what he kept in there.

When she saw the contents she froze, sinking to the reclining chair in the corner of the bedroom with the box in her hands. In the drawer was a pile of photographs, six of them, held together with an elastic band. They were all of her.

The top one she remembered, a candid shot taken when she was laughing at Maddy's antics at a Halloween party. Under it were four others, showing various poses, including the proof for her junior yearbook photo. And at the back of the pack she found a five-by-seven of the two of them, snapped by Jack's sister Lalage when they spent a stolen evening at his house. It was captioned, in Jack's hand, Jesse and Me, Last Date.

It was true. That was the final time they had been together, shortly before her fatal visit to Dr. Carstairs. Jessica sat staring at the photos, thinking that he had put them together after she was gone, to remember her. He had kept them all these years in this box with his most personal things, a testament to his depth of feeling for the girl who had left him behind.

Jessica closed her eyes, the pictures falling to the floor as she put her hands to her face. If he had felt so strongly about her once, why couldn't he love her now, when they had a second chance? Why was he wasting it on a vengeance that was surely destroying them both? There was no understanding his baffling complexity, his stubborn adherence to a stance that was creating such unhappiness. Even today, when he might have comforted her at the hospital, let her see that he was glad she was all right, he had gone back to work and left her alone. She sat in a trance for several minutes, then gathered up the photos and put them away, making sure to replace the box where she had found it. She hadn't meant to pry, but it wouldn't do to reveal that she had discovered his secret.

By the time Jack came home from work that evening, Jessica had showered and was brushing her hair. He paused in the doorway of the bedroom, watching her work through the silken mass methodically, and then came to stand behind her, taking the brush from her hand without a word. Jessica bent her head as he brushed her hair till it crackled, using long, powerful strokes that made her scalp tingle and turned the individual strands into threads of the finest gossamer. When she looked up, he had gathered them into his fist, lifting the weight off her neck. Her eyes met his in the vanity mirror, and a current passed between them. Jessica waited for his next move, but he chose to turn away, letting her hair fall back into place and tossing the brush onto her enameled tray. Jessica let her breath out slowly as he went to change, thinking that he delighted in refusing her slightest invitation. The message was brutally clear: it always had to be his idea.

She dressed carefully in a deep emerald evening dress, fitted and strapless, with a long side slit designed to reveal one graceful leg. She had bought it the week before, at the urging of both Jean and the saleswoman, when Jessica herself had thought it too dramatic, too revealing. But one look at Jack's face when she emerged from the bedroom wearing it convinced her that her advisers had been correct.

"You look beautiful," he said flatly, and Jessica wondered wearily why he never sounded happy when he gave her a compliment. It was almost as if he resented the ascendancy her beauty gave her over his will and emotions, and so viewed her physical allure with guarded respect, with meticulous caution.

He didn't look bad himself. The black tuxedo flattered his lean, muscular frame and the pleated, stark white shirt set off his dark good looks to perfection, making his hair and eyes lustrous, vivid. They were, indeed, an attractive couple, and Jessica wondered how many people viewing the handsome newlyweds that evening could guess at the turmoil concealed by their sartorial splendor.

Jack went to the hall closet and got her long evening cloak of soft, brushed wool, hooded and lined with fur. He slipped it over her shoulders and the folds swirled around her ankles. He put his topcoat over his arm and they went out to the elevator and descended to his car.

The chamber of commerce had rented a local club for the event. It was ablaze with lights and decorations as Jack and Jessica arrived. The carpeted entry hall had a twenty-foot Christmas tree decorated in blue and silver, with a myriad of tiny winking stars set among its branches. The crowd milled around in its shadow, greeting friends, checking coats and lining up to enter the ballroom. Jessica hoped it was her imagination that a hush seemed to fall over the gathering as she and Jack passed through it. She was relieved to see that Maddy and her husband were already seated.

Soon after they joined their table, the chairman of the event rose from the dais to speak. As she listened to him describe the wonderful things in store for the museum, Jessica looked around for Daphne, who was sure to be present. The chairman outlined the planned allocation of funds raised from this event, the various committees formed and their duties, while Jessica scanned the crowd, searching for Daphne's dark, curly head. She finally gave up and was settling back in her seat when she looked right into Daphne's eyes. The other woman was watching her, not ten feet away, and Jessica, startled, gave her a weak smile. Daphne smiled back, nodding, and on the pretext of listening to the speech Jessica shifted in her chair to face the front of the room, breathing a silent sigh of resignation. Daphne was at the next table. Jessica looked at Jack, who was paying attention to the talk and had missed the wordless exchange. She looked down at her hands and resolved to stop acting like a skittish ten-year-old. When the chairman sat down she applauded politely as if she actually knew what he had said.

The dinner was the usual marginally edible fare served at such events. At the break before dessert the band began to play old standards, and a large portion of the crowd got up to dance. Daphne seized the first opportunity for conversation and appeared at Jessica's side, her expression mischievous.

"Aren't you the sly fox?" she said, glancing sidelong at Jack. "Showing up out of the blue and stealing Jack here away from us."

Us? Jessica thought. Who is us?

"I'm sorry about what happened when I called," Daphne went on to say. "I didn't realize who I was talking to. I didn't know about your wedding."

"That's all right," Jessica said faintly, wishing Daphne weren't quite so magnanimous about the whole thing. Her deliberate cheerfulness was giving Jessica a headache.

"You should have told me who you were," Daphne bubbled. "You could have knocked me over with a feather when I heard."

I'll bet, Jessica thought.

"We have a lot to catch up on," Daphne confided, pulling her empty chair next to Jessica's and sliding into it. "What have you been doing with yourself since you left Bright River?"

Jack was watching the two of them with a set, expressionless face. As Jessica tried to give Daphne a heavily edited version of her activities over the past decade, Jack turned to Maddy's husband and engaged him in conversation. Maddy observed the scene with her usual wry detachment, wondering why these people weren't attacking each other.

Daphne burbled on about this and that, as Jessica prayed for deliverance. She knew Jack wouldn't save her; he wouldn't get between them for a crock of gold. Jessica tried to listen, smiling until she felt her face would crack. The worst part about it was that she actually liked Daphne, always had. But the sight of her, beautifully dressed in a black crepe décolleté gown, conjured up images of what she had been doing in bed with Jack not too long ago, and was probably still doing with him now. Jack was gone a lot, and he never gave an explanation for his absences.

A man loomed behind Daphne's chair, and it took Jessica a moment to recognize him. When she did, she greeted him as if he were about to lead her out of the desert and into the promised land.

"Bill!" she exclaimed, standing and seizing his hand. "Bill Campbell, it's wonderful to see you. How have you been?"

"Great, Jessica," Bill said. "How about yourself? I understand you just married our football star over here."

Jack stood to shake hands with Bill, who had been in Jessica's class at school. She'd always liked him, a sunny, friendly boy whose father was a local postman.

"Aren't you going to ask me to dance?" Jessica said to him, desperate to get away from the table. Bill, who looked a little surprised by the suggestion, nevertheless took her arm with commendable gallantry and led her onto the floor.

They hadn't been dancing a minute when Bill said to her, "Jessica, what's the matter with you?"

"Why do you ask?" Jessica replied, as if he had no basis for the question.

"You were never the type to ask a man to dance. You've either changed a whole lot, or something's up. Which is it?"

"Something's up," Jessica admitted, surrendering. "I just wanted to get away from Daphne. She was asking me so many questions."

"Daphne's my date," Bill replied, grinning.

Jessica closed her eyes. "I'm sorry," she said helplessly.

"It's all right," Bill said, laughing. "I know what she's like. I also know she was seeing Jack right up until the time he married you. Uncomfortable situation, huh?"

"You might say that."

"Is she a sore loser?"

"No, no at all. She was trying to be cordial, I think, but oh, I guess it's me. Don't pay any attention. Daphne's nice and I don't mean to imply otherwise."

"Don't worry about saying anything wrong to me. I take her to these things about three times a year because we're both involved in local business. That's all it is."

Jessica had a brief flash of sympathy for Daphne. She seemed to be rather commonly regarded as a good time. "I didn't know you worked in town," Jessica said brightly, trying to change the subject.

"Yes, when my parents died I sold the house and opened an appliance outlet. Maybe you've seen it? Red C Discounters."

"That's your place?" Jessica said. "I've driven past it, but I didn't realize you owned it."

"Yeah, I've been there about four years." Bill went on to tell her about his business, and when Jessica glanced back at the table she saw that both Jack and Daphne were missing. Sure enough, they were dancing together on the opposite side of the room. And it seemed to Jessica that Jack was holding the other woman very close. Suddenly she didn't feel like dancing anymore.

"I'd like to sit down, Bill, if you don't mind," she said.

"Sure," replied Bill, confused but gallant. She reached her chair in time to see Jack laughing with Daphne.

He'd be better off with her, Jessica thought sadly. He would relax, take it easy. Not sweat the small stuff the way he does with me. This perception did nothing to enhance her evening.

"See you later," Bill said, undoubtedly relieved to get away from her. He walked back to his table as Maddy leaned across the floral centerpiece and whispered, "Why did you bolt like that? You left your husband free for the black dahlia to lasso him into a dance."

"I'm sure she didn't have to try very hard," Jessica murmured.

Maddy was making a face at her when Jack returned Daphne to Bill, and then rejoined his table. Maddy's husband immediately resumed their conversation, a rehash of some football game Jack had won with a last-minute touchdown. Several other men came over to join the discussion, and as Jessica listened to Jack's amusing recounting of the crucial play, she smiled along with the others. She had almost forgotten how truly charming he could be. He was so wired around her that his natural personality was submerged and lost in the general tension. In a situation like this he could be open, outgoing, funny. Surely this was part of the reason she had fallen in love with him in the first place, but she no longer remembered the process. She had long accepted her love for him as a condition of existence, like rain or the change of seasons. Snow fell, the sun rose and she loved Jack. But now she could see that he was happier away from her. Wasn't she selfish to cling to something that distorted, almost negated, his true nature?

"I'm going for some air," Jessica announced to Maddy, rising from her seat. Maddy, who knew that it was twelve degrees outside, looked at her suspiciously.

"Just into the hall," Jessica clarified, and before Maddy could respond she left, weaving through the crowd to the large entry foyer, which was almost deserted. She sat on one of the couches flanking the coatroom, inhaling the cooler air admitted by the frequent opening of the outer doors. The ballroom, filled with body heat and cigarette smoke, had been stifling.

She was trying hard to refute the evidence of her eyes, but she was failing. She could see that Jack was different with other people; when not around her he became the Jack she remembered from their youth. The only way to allow him to be himself, to be content, was to leave him.

Tears squeezed from under her lids and ran down her face. She wiped at them hastily as she heard footsteps behind her and turned to look at Bill, who was standing before the cloakroom with a check stub in his hand.

"Jessica?" he said, shoving the stub into his pocket and sitting next to her, peering into her face. "Have you been crying?"

She couldn't deny it, and suddenly the whole evening overwhelmed her. To her own horror she began to sob. Bill's arm came around her immediately, and he held her head against his shoulder.

"There, there," he said soothingly, as if comforting a child. "Has Daphne been at you again? She just told me she wanted to leave. It wasn't because you two had a fight, was it?"

Jessica shook her head, unable to speak. He patted her back awkwardly, at a loss.

"Campbell," Jack said in icy tones behind them, "I think you'd better take your hands off my wife."

Nine

Jessica and Bill sprang apart immediately. Jessica took one look at Jack's face and leaped to her feet, putting herself between the two men.

"Jack, listen to me," she said hastily as Jack advanced, his expression thunderous. "You don't understand."

"I understand, all right," Jack responded tightly, balling his hands into fists. "You leave me alone at the table to sneak out here and meet this guy. When I come after you I find you in his arms."

"That isn't what happened at all!" Bill interjected, and Jack took another step toward him. Jessica planted herself in his path, determined to protect poor Bill, who was only trying to help her.

"Jack, you are acting like a child," she said, her mood changing to indignation.

"I don't want to tell you what you're acting like, necking on a settee with this bozo while I'm looking all over for you."

"I was not necking on a settee!" she fired back. Bill, who was certain now that they were *both* ready to be institutionalized, was edging toward the door.

"Get back here, you!" Jack roared, pushing Jessica aside.

Jessica grabbed his arm, hanging on so that he would have to hurt her to be rid of her.

"Jack, if you make a scene here I will never forgive you," she said quietly, trembling with anger, her lips white.

From the safety of the vestibule, Bill called out, "I would listen to her, if I were you, Chabrol. And while you're at it, I would ask your bride why she was running away from the crowd in there to come outside and cry by herself." He went out and slammed the door, leaving Jessica and Jack to stare at each other.

"Is that true?" Jack asked. "Were you crying?"

He was genuinely upset; his accent was back, transforming "were" into "where."

"Why are you asking me?" Jessica replied. "I thought you had everything all figured out."

"Well, what would you have thought if you'd seen what I did?" he countered.

"I might have paused to ask a question!" she answered, but she knew that wasn't true. If she had seen Jack in a similar situation with Daphne, she would have drawn the same conclusion.

"We're leaving," he said abruptly.

"Fine," Jessica said, turning her back on him.

He went back inside, making some excuse for their abrupt departure, and then returned to bundle Jessica into her wrap and hustle her out to the car.

The night was bitter cold. The drive back was conducted without heat, as Jack wouldn't wait for the engine to warm up. He pushed the sports car through the empty streets, grinding the gears as he took the turns. The forecast was for snow, and it hung heavy in the night sky, masking the stars. They didn't say a word to each other as they ascended to the apartment. Jack turned on the lights and tossed his keys on the dining table before he whirled to face her.

"All right," he said tightly. "Why don't you tell me what that little scene with Campbell was all about?"

"He already did tell you. Bill came out and found me when I was...upset. You saw him comforting me, that's all."

"You didn't plan to meet him there?" Jack demanded.

"Of course not," Jessica replied wearily. "Why on earth would you think that?"

"Why not? You were wrapped around him all night."

Jessica glared at him, astonished. "Jack, I danced with him *once*."

"That's more than you danced with me!" he flung back at her, his hands on his hips.

"How was I supposed to dance with you? I would have needed a crowbar to pry you apart from your mistress!" It was out before she could stop it, and Jessica was sickened by the tortured, helpless jealousy she heard in her own voice.

Jack's expression became guarded. "My mistress?" he said cautiously.

"You don't suppose I believed that you were working during all those evenings you left me alone, do you?" she asked miserably.

His face went blank. He *had* been working, and it had never occurred to him that she might suspect otherwise. All

this time that he had shared her bed she'd been thinking he
was sharing another one with Daphne. And she had never
said a word, even though he could see that the idea of it
tormented her.

"You thought I was with Daphne?" he said slowly,
buying time.

"You told me you wouldn't give her up."

His thoughts flashed back to the argument they'd had
the day after their marriage. He must have given her that
impression, but he had been striking out recklessly, saying anything he guessed would hurt. The truth was that
he'd forgotten Daphne the minute he knew Jesse was back
in town, but he wasn't going to tell her that.

"You have no right to accuse me," he said softly, still
stalling, his mind racing to consider the implications of
what she was saying.

"That's true," she replied, nodding. "I have no rights
at all, isn't that the arrangement?" Her eyes misted over
and her lower lip trembled. "You just had to bring me
there tonight and force me to see her, didn't you? You
wanted to rub my nose in it."

His gaze grew intent and his voice got even quieter. "Is
that why you were crying?" he asked, taking a step forward and seizing her in a viselike grip.

Jessica tried to pull loose. It was like trying to shake off
a boa constrictor.

"Tell me," he insisted. "Is that why you were crying?"

"What difference does it make to you?" she hedged, her
pride coming to the fore, unwilling to admit that his involvement with Daphne had wounded her so deeply.

"What difference does it make?" he said hoarsely. "Do
you think I can forget for one moment that I bought you
like chattel? That if you had any choice in the matter you
wouldn't be with me?"

Jessica stared up at him, her pulses racing, afraid to answer. He sounded as if he really cared, as if he wanted her to reciprocate a feeling he already had for her. Terrified that the hopes he was raising would be dashed, she caught him unaware and slipped out of his grasp, whirling away from him. He lunged after her, and the high heel of her slipper caught on the edge of the rug, sending her tumbling to the floor.

Jack was on his knees beside her in a second. He reached for her, and she flinched from him.

He drew back, his face registering shock. "You're afraid of me, aren't you?" he asked in a low, emotionless tone.

She didn't answer, looking away.

He sat back on his haunches, putting his face in his hands. "Oh, God," he murmured almost inaudibly, barely loud enough for her to hear, "how did we come to this?" He looked up, and Jessica was chilled by the expression of bleak desolation in his eyes. "Do you remember how happy we once were?"

"I remember," she replied softly.

He reached out and touched her face. "Are you all right?" he asked, cupping her chin in his hand and turning her face up to the light.

"Of course. I just tripped."

He pulled her against his chest, and she didn't even think of resisting.

"My Jesse," he whispered, his lips moving in her hair. "I wish we could wipe away the years and go back to that last fall we had together."

"If only that were possible, Jack."

"Let me try," he muttered. "Let me try to take us both back." He stood, picking her up in his arms and it seemed the most natural thing in the world that he should carry her to the bed.

Jack set her down gently, letting her slip back into the softness of the pillows, and then turned her over and unzipped the velvet dress. She was naked above the waist, and he pulled aside the panels of the gown, leaving her uncovered to the base of her spine. Jessica lay unmoving, prone, waiting for what he would do. She sensed his nearness and then felt the touch of his lips trailing lightly over her back, pressing into the dimpled hollows below her shoulder blades. She shivered, and he ran his hands up her bare arms, lifting her toward him. The dress fell away, and he reached around her, cupping her breasts. Jessica sighed with gratification as he mouthed her nape, then slid one arm across her torso to hold her steady and caressed her freely with his other hand.

"Your skin is the softest I've ever touched," he murmured, tonguing her ear. "I never forgot the feel of it."

Jessica turned in his arms, reaching up to lock her hands behind his head. He bent and kissed her lingeringly, with steadily gathering intensity, until he was crushing her to him fiercely. He drew her into his lap, tugging off her skirt and slip, and then slipped an arm beneath her knees, cradling her as he laved the valley between her breasts with his tongue. Jessica lay back against his shoulder, her eyes closed, her lips parted, while he made love to her. Her nipples stiffened under his skillful attention, blossoming into rosy buds, and when he drew back to remove her panties she arched up to help him.

"You are beautiful," he whispered, dipping his head to kiss the slight swell of her belly as he settled her onto the bed. Then he straightened and reached for the top button of his shirt.

Jessica put her hand over his. "Let me," she said softly, removing the studs one by one until she could ease her fingers into the opening she'd created and slide them over his chest. Jack sat immobile, letting her fondle him, his eyes slitted, his expression rapt. She peeled the heavy linen shirt from his shoulders and let it fall to the bed, moving up on one elbow to press her mouth to a broad, flat nipple. He inhaled sharply as she trailed her tongue down the line of dark hair to his belt, and then paused to undo it.

He stiffened, and she whispered, "I want to make love to you."

He had never allowed this, and she waited for him to push her away as he'd done in the past. But he helped her take off the rest of his clothes, and when she finally encircled him with a tentative, exploring touch, he was lost. He closed his eyes and fell back on his elbows, enduring the exquisite torment of her searching hands until she bent to kiss him. He moaned helplessly, conquered where he would have been the conqueror, and opened his eyes to look into hers as she raised her head.

But Jessica was not finished. She pushed him farther backward until he was lying down and then laid her cheek against his hard thigh, her arms encircling his hips.

Jack froze, waiting, until at last she moved, touching him with the tip of her tongue. He gasped and put one hand on the back of her head, urging her onward. He was silent as she caressed him, and then, groaning with a desire so intense he felt engulfed by it, he seized her upper arms and lifted her onto him.

Jessica gasped with the exquisite sensation as she fell forward, her palms flat against his shoulders. He tugged on her hair, and she tilted her head back to look at him.

"I never wanted any woman the way I want you," he rasped, his eyes closing luxuriously as he ran his hands down her back and shifted her weight, moving deeper within her. Jessica kissed his lashes, damp and bristling against her lips, and his flushed cheek, rough with stub-

ble. When she reached his mouth, it opened for her, and
she slid her hands over the broad expanse of his shoulders
as he responded, giving himself, with tenderness, more
freely than he had since they were married. This was the
first time he had spoken to her during the act of love, and
she knew this was a breakthrough. She could feel the
change, in him, in herself. As they surged forward, lost in
each other, she thought, This time he'll hold me afterward. I know he will.

And he did.

Jessica awoke to find herself alone in the bed, and at
first she couldn't believe it. She'd really thought that he
would stay. They had fallen asleep with her still curled
against him, and she hadn't felt him leave. Her disappointment was so deep that it drove her out into the hall to
look for him, pulling on her robe with unsteady hands. But
when she walked into the guest room she halted, seeing
that the bed was empty. He was gone, not just from her
bed, but from the apartment.

She glanced at the clock and felt an abrupt stab of fear.
It was three o'clock in the morning and one of the coldest
nights of the year. Where had he gone?

Jessica was certain that she would not be able to sleep
and put the kettle on to make herself a cup of tea.

One word kept forming over and over in her conscious-
ness: why? Why had he run away again when she was sure,
after that last hour in bed, that they had a chance? She
knew she had not imagined what had happened between
them. Had it frightened him, threatened his need for vengeance and caused his resolve to weaken? What was going
on in his mind? He was so complex, so unpredictable, that
he could be thinking anything.

Jessica drew aside the living room curtain and looked down at the deserted street. A light snow had begun to fall, and it blanketed the asphalt with a thin layer of white. She turned away as the kettle whistled shrilly and went to the kitchen. As she got out a mug and a tea bag she thought that she couldn't take much more of this and hoped that he would return safely, and quickly, before she lost hope altogether.

Jack slid his glass across the bar and said, "Give me another one of those, will you, Bob?"

"Sure thing, Jack," the bartender said. He poured a second shot into the tumbler and said, "Looks like we're in for some weather tonight."

"Yeah, it was starting to snow as I came in."

The man examined him for several seconds and then said, "You mind if I ask you a question?"

"Go ahead," Jack replied, downing the contents of his glass in one gulp.

"What are you doing here?"

"I'm here because this is the only bar open till four a.m.," Jack responded, wiping his mouth with the back of his hand.

"No, I mean, why are you out at all? I heard you just got married."

Jack sat quietly for a moment and then said, "I did."

Bob arched his brows. "Is it true you married Jessica Portman?"

Jack nodded, not looking up.

The man shook his head. "Boy, I remember her. You were three years ahead of me in school, and she was two, I guess. But you couldn't miss her. She sure was a looker."

"She sure was," Jack whispered.

"Still is, I guess?" the man ventured.

"Still is," Jack confirmed softly.

"She disappeared there for a while, was out of the country or something, but she's not the type you forget."

"No."

Bob grinned. "She was probably trying to get away from her father, the old codger. You ever see him?"

"Not now."

"I worked one summer in his factory, you know, filling in for the regulars. He drove everybody like he was carrying a whip. I never could understand how something as sweet as Jessica could be his daughter."

"I think she's like her mother," Jack said.

"I saw in the paper the old man was real sick."

Jack met the other man's eyes, turning his empty glass in his fingers. "He's in a nursing home."

Bob's expression changed. "Gee, I'm sorry to hear that. For your wife, I mean. I can't say I have much feeling for the guy himself. He was not exactly what you'd call likable."

Jack didn't answer. The statement did not require a response.

"So how long you been married?" Bob asked, wiping down the bar. He was killing time until closing, and Jack was the only remaining patron.

"Two months."

"Then I have to repeat myself. Why are you sitting here talking to me when you could be home with your gorgeous bride?"

"That's a very good question," Jack observed.

"Is she away or something?"

"She's back at my apartment."

Bob stared at him. "Look, buddy, it's none of my business, but . . ."

Jack stood abruptly. "You're right. It's none of your business."

Bob watched him fishing for money in his pocket. He had been a bartender too long to pay attention to anything a drinker said. "You going home?" he asked mildly, as Jack produced a wad of bills and tossed several on the counter before him.

"Are you my mother?" Jack countered, glaring at him.

Bob held up his hand in a gesture of appeasement. "Hey, don't take offense. I just can't figure you out, that's all. A guy like you, you got everything. You shouldn't be risking it all, drinking, driving around in the snow in the middle of the night."

Jack smiled thinly, turning up his collar. Yes, he had everything, including a beautiful wife he had purchased like an addition to a harem, coldly, bloodlessly, because she wouldn't have come to him willingly. He was Jack Chabrol, superstar, and he could take what he wanted. Wasn't that his right? Wasn't that what he'd learned in four years of pro football, that money was power, and if you had enough of it you could make people do anything? You could even get a young, desirable woman to stay with you when she didn't want to, because your money could take care of her invalid father and send her kid sister to school. Oh, there was a lot for him to be grateful for, proud of, no doubt about it.

He realized that Bob was talking to him. "What did you say?"

"I asked if you wanted me to call you a cab."

Jack shook his head. "No, thanks, Bob, I'm not drunk. I only wish I was."

"G'night, then."

"Good night," Jack responded. "Forget what I said before. I'm not in the best of moods tonight."

"It's forgotten. Say hello to your wife for me. Tell her Bob Randall. My sister Kim was in her class."

"I will." Jack headed for the door as Bob looked after him, thinking that you just didn't know about people. Jack Chabrol, with all his looks and money, his booming business, his pretty new wife, was not a happy man. Maybe he didn't have everything after all.

Jack walked out into the cold, blustery night and jammed his hands into his pockets. The snow sifted over his face and settled on his shoulders as he walked to his car, thinking that he couldn't put it off a minute longer. He would have to go back to Jessica and tell her what he had decided. He couldn't compel her to participate in this farce anymore. Her persistent kindness and patience had driven away his desire for revenge and left in its place a longing for the love he knew she could never give him.

Jack leaned against the closed door of his car and stared up at the frigid moon, partially visible behind a hazy bank of swollen clouds. The ancients believed the moon induced madness, and he almost felt as if he'd been under a spell where Jesse was concerned. He was not normally cruel, but he'd treated her cruelly. He'd rejected her every overture of normal companionship, dealing with her as if she were a hooker he kept in his house for the sake of convenience. She had only been trying to do her best with the bad situation he had forced on her, and he'd purposely made it almost impossible for her to hang on to any shred of self-respect. Not to mention plotting and executing the downfall of her family fortunes just to render her vulnerable to his attack in the first place. It *was* madness, and it was going to stop, tonight.

It was amazing how easy it actually was, in the end. All he had to do was finally confess to himself what he had stubbornly denied all along: that he still loved Jesse, had always loved her. The admission was liberating. Having faced the truth, he could let her go. He'd been using the past as an excuse to hold her, and the constant effort necessary to sustain the fiction had exhausted him. Better to release her and let her forget, even if he knew he never could.

Jack unlocked the door of his car and got behind the wheel, staring straight ahead, hardly feeling the cold as he tried to start the engine. It took three attempts to get it going, and then it coughed into life. The delicate Italian machinery, suited to a warmer climate, was having some trouble coming to grips with the weather. He waited until the car warmed up, not anxious to begin the trip, and then headed home, driving slowly because of the snow and his own growing sense of dread.

When he entered the apartment the first thing he saw was Jessica sitting on the couch, her legs curled under her, staring at the door. She straightened alertly, saying, "Jack, thank God. I was so worried."

He walked to the love seat facing her and sat on its edge, not bothering to remove his coat. The snowflakes were melting in his hair, creating little spots of wetness in the sable waves, and he looked haggard, his beard rough and dark.

"I'm glad you're awake," he said. "I have to talk to you."

Ten

I couldn't sleep," Jessica replied, preoccupied with his serious, almost relieved air. He looked like a man who had come to a difficult conclusion, but was now glad the thinking period was over.

"Oh, no?" he said, pushing his damp hair back from his forehead.

"I woke up and you were gone, Jack. It was the middle of the night and I didn't know where you were."

"I see. Well, I'm sorry you were concerned, but we might as well get this over with now," he said.

"Get what over with?" Jessica asked. "Jack, what are you talking about?" A chill, like a cold mist, was moving in around her heart. She knew she wasn't going to like what was coming.

He looked at her for a moment, into her eyes, and then glanced away. His throat was working, and his big hands hung uselessly as he said, "I'm not going to hold you to this anymore, Jesse. You can have a divorce whenever you want."

Jessica was stunned into silence. Just hours before she had been thinking of leaving him. But that was before their last time together. Evidently the thing that had convinced her they might have a chance had only convinced him that they didn't.

He kept staring into the distance as he went on. "I'll still cover your father's care until he's on his feet and Jean's education. You don't have to pay me back. God knows you've earned the money, enduring what I've put you through these past couple of months. And once the house is renovated you can have it as part of the settlement, as well as any alimony you think fair. I'm sure Ransom can set it up whatever way you want."

Jessica could tell by the way he spoke that he had given the arrangements a great deal of consideration. He must have been sitting someplace for hours, mulling it over, deciding how he could cut her loose as painlessly as possible. He obviously thought that if he gave her everything anyone could possibly want she wouldn't fight him.

He must be very eager to be rid of her. She felt her throat tighten with the constriction of oncoming tears and swallowed hard, forcing them back. She seemed to spend a good deal of her time bawling lately, but she wasn't going to do it now. She would be brave if it killed her.

Jack still hadn't turned to her, and he went on talking in a dull monotone, as if he had rehearsed this speech and had to get it all out before he forgot it or lost his nerve. "I know you don't want me," he said expressionlessly. "You did once. I felt that you did, even if you went along with what your father said in the end. This time it was different. I used the only leverage I had, leverage I had created, to get you." He sighed heavily, his shoulders slumping.

"But you can't recapture a memory. I'm sorry I gave you such a bad time." He stopped, as if to phrase his next thoughts more carefully.

Jessica no longer felt like crying. She was sitting bolt upright, her eyes riveted on his face, her fingers knotted in her lap. Could he possibly be saying what she thought he was saying?

"You left me," she whispered, blurting out the first idea she could articulate. "Every time we made love, you left me. You always slept in the other bedroom."

"I was afraid to stay, afraid that we would both see how I really felt," he murmured.

"Every time?" she asked softly, barely breathing.

"Every time. I felt so close to you afterward, and I just knew that if I stayed, I would not be able to shut you out."

"Oh, Jack," she murmured. How had she misunderstood so completely?

He stood abruptly, his back to her. "Please don't feel sorry for me," he said tightly.

"Jack, wait . . ."

He made a silencing gesture. "Just let me get this out," he directed curtly, and she allowed him to continue. There would be all the time in the world for her to say her piece when he was finished. A quiet sort of joy was welling up within her, filling her with the certainty that no matter what he told her now, everything would be all right.

"You may not believe this, and I wouldn't blame you if you didn't, but I love you," he said quietly, looking at her for the first time. "Now more than ever, and I loved you more than life itself when we were kids. All those years we were apart, every time I got close to another woman, I saw your face. I was engaged once, did you know that? But I couldn't go through with it. She was a nice girl, but she just wasn't . . . you. I wound up hurting her because I let it get too far before I saw the truth and called it off. I wanted to feel about her the way I had about you, and I didn't. And if I couldn't have that, I didn't want anything. I told myself that the feeling I remembered happened only because we were so young, and I repeated it so often I guess I came to believe it. And when you came back, all I could focus on was the hate for what you'd done, for the way you'd left me. I wouldn't see the truth, that the emotions didn't have anything to do with age or maturity. It was you. You were the only person who could make me feel that way."

Jessica sat watching him, her eyes huge, the fingertips of one hand pressed to her lips, as if to stem the tide of words that threatened to rush out at him. She kept silent with an effort. She had waited a long time for this, wondering how he really felt, and she wanted to hear it all. Now that he had begun, she could see that he was loath to stop. He raced ahead, unloading the burden of pain and uncertainty he had carried since his youth. And through it all, a refrain kept repeating in Jessica's brain: he loves me, he said he loves me.

"This is tough," he said huskily, clearing his throat. "Even now I'm tempted to ask you to stay with me, to give it another try. I don't care anymore about how or why you left; I don't know if I ever really did. Maybe it was all an excuse to keep you with me, pretending it was for revenge, while in reality I just couldn't bear to let you go. You can make yourself believe anything if you want something badly enough, and I wanted you real bad." He coughed. "Anyway, I won't plead with you to keep on with this. I know how miserable you've been, and to tell you the truth, it's been hell for me too, seeing you so unhappy every day. I thought I was hardened enough to take anything, but that has about done me in. So it's best we call it quits. You can't force these things." He looked down at the floor, and added in an unsteady voice, "I'm sure you'd like children, and I know you wouldn't want *my* children." He stopped short, and Jessica realized that he was too upset to go on. She couldn't have kept quiet any longer anyway. Listening to him on this subject was too much to take in silence.

"I do want your children, Jack," she said softly, and she was amazed at how controlled she sounded as she finally told him what she had longed for him to know for ten years. "I wanted your child that last winter we were together. That's why I left Bright River."

It was several seconds before he raised his head, and she saw dawning comprehension in his eyes as he gazed at her.

"What do you mean?" he asked in a deadly quiet voice. He had gone pale, and he was staring at her with an intensity that made her feel transparent.

"I was pregnant with your child, Jack. My father told me that if I didn't marry a man he knew, a man he considered suitable to be my husband and the father of his grandchild, he would prosecute you for statutory rape."

Jack simply looked at her, dumbstruck.

"He would have done it, too. And you had no possible defense. You were over eighteen and I was underage. The consent of the minor doesn't negate the charge, and the district attorney was in his pocket. They were buddies. He left me no choice. So I did what he told me to do. I went to New York and married his friend. After my miscarriage I divorced him and never came back here until my father fell ill."

Jack sat down heavily, as if his legs would not support him. When he finally spoke his voice sounded rusty, unused.

"Why didn't you tell me this when you came back two months ago?"

Jessica smiled sadly. "And let you ruin my father?"

He searched her face, and then closed his eyes. The gesture was an admission of responsibility for everything that had followed her return.

"Anyway, I thought that even if I told you I was pregnant when I left that January, you would have said the child was Arthur's."

"Arthur's?" he repeated woodenly.

"Arthur was the man I married. My father told you I had been seeing him while I was with you, didn't he?"

Jack eyed her miserably, and nodded. "He never said the name, only that you'd had another boyfriend in New York, and you'd left town to marry him."

"I was sure it was something of the kind. Can't you see that he said that because, with your background and insecurities, you'd believe it? There was never anyone else, Jack. The baby was yours."

"And you lost it?" he asked huskily.

"Yes."

He bent his head and covered his face with his hands. "Oh, Jesse, the awful things I said to you," he rasped, his voice muffled. "How can you ever forgive me?"

"I forgave you when you said them. It was your pain talking, I know that."

"And the way I've treated you since we've been married?" he asked, lifting his head and eyeing her warily, as if she might strike him.

"You have the rest of our lives to make up for that," she said gently. "Starting right now."

"Are you saying..." he began hoarsely, then paused to take a deep breath and start again. "Are you saying that you'll stay with me?"

"Of course, Jack. I love you. Where else would I go?"

He rose suddenly, and as she watched in astonishment, headed for the door. As soon as she divined his intention she called after him, "I'm telling you right now, Jacques, if you leave me again you are going to be in big trouble."

He halted in his tracks and turned into the bedroom instead, slamming the door after him. Jessica heard him lock it. She waited a decent interval, and then knocked softly.

"Jack, let me in, I want to talk to you."

No response.

"Jack, please. Don't shut me out. We've wasted too much time already at cross purposes."

She heard the lock give and the door swung inward. As she crossed the threshold she saw him sitting in the shadows. He wouldn't look at her.

"Jack, don't try to handle this alone," she whispered, standing in front of him and putting her hand on his shoulder. In the next second he had pulled her into his arms and pressed his face to her breast. She held him and stroked his hair as if he were a little boy.

"I feel like such a damn fool," he said huskily when he could talk. "Why did I listen to him, when I knew how much he hated me, how much he wanted to tear us apart?"

She understood that he was talking about her father. "You were only a kid, Jack, and he was a smart man with a wide experience of the world. He knew just what to say. I don't blame you. Don't blame yourself."

"I do," he murmured. "I always will, for the years we've lost."

"We're still young. We can start again."

He drew back and looked up at her from his sitting position. "Can we?" he asked quietly. His eyes sought hers for guidance. His customary air of authority and competence was gone.

"I'm counting on it," Jessica replied, smoothing his hair.

He turned his head as her hand fell to his cheek and he kissed it. "Jesse," he whispered. "Why didn't you find me after you lost the baby? Why did you wait so long?"

"I wrote Maddy from Europe after I got settled there with my job, and she told me you were away at school. It seemed you had gone on without me. I didn't want to intrude on your life again."

"Intrude?" he said incredulously. "I was lost without you. How could you think otherwise?"

"I was hurt by all of it, too, Jack," Jessica replied softly. "I wasn't reasoning clearly. The only thing I knew was that I had to get away from my father and what he had done. I ran so far I left the country."

"I'm sorry," he said hastily, standing and enfolding her. "Of course you were hurt, I can only imagine what you must have suffered. It's just that I keep thinking about the days and weeks and months we threw away, playing right into your father's hands."

"Do you still hate him?" Jessica asked, snuggling against his chest.

"I did. I used to hate him so much I could have killed him. But I don't know after all this time. I'm kind of worn out with it, you know? It's like the only thing that matters is that you left me back then in order to protect me, not because you preferred a rich man that your father liked."

"I'm so glad," Jessica murmured. "If you could see him now, how beaten and resigned he is, you wouldn't be able to feel anything but pity, believe me. Maddy said something about people paying for the wrong they do. I wonder if it's true. Every time I see him, I think it is."

"Does Maddy know all about this?" Jack asked.

"Yes, I told her."

Jack sighed, tightening his grip on her. "She must think I'm a horse's ass."

Jessica giggled. "Since when do you care what Maddy thinks? You were always dodging her when we were in school."

"She's your friend," Jack said archly. "I don't want her bad-mouthing me to you."

"As if I'd listen," Jessica sniffed.

"Aha! So she's tried."

"Well, she expressed an opinion or two."

He held her at arm's length. "Like what?"

"She said you married me in indecent haste."

He grinned, and Jessica's heart turned over. She hadn't seen that smile, a real smile, since that last evening when Lalage took their picture, the one she'd found in his valet box.

"She's right about that," he responded. "I couldn't wait to get you into bed." Then his expression changed. He bent suddenly and slipped one arm under her knees and swung her off the floor.

"Jack, what are you doing?" she protested as he marched out of the bedroom and into the hall with her in his arms.

"I just remembered something," he said, opening the outer door of the apartment and stepping into the corridor.

"Am I going to find out what it is?" she asked. "I hate to point this out to you, but it's about five in the morning, and I'm wearing nothing but a semitransparent robe."

"I wish you were wearing nothing," he said, nuzzling her neck and pulling the door shut behind them.

"If any of your neighbors are up, they're going to think this performance very strange."

"They're all asleep, and if they're not, the hell with them," Jack replied, opening the door again and carrying her back inside.

"Is this supposed to signify something?" Jessica asked, as he reentered the apartment and deposited her on the floor.

"I carried you across the threshold," he explained. "I never did it when we came back from the wedding. I thought you might punch me if I tried."

"Punch you? Never."

"Well, you weren't exactly cooperative about the rest of the arrangements. No reception, no honey..." He snapped his fingers. "The honeymoon! We have to have one now. Where would you like to go?"

"I'll go anywhere with you, Mr. Chabrol."

"That's reassuring, Mrs. Chabrol, but not very informative. How does Hawaii sound? It might be nice to ditch all this cold weather."

"Hawaii sounds wonderful. But unless I've been misinformed, the only requirements for a honeymoon are two people and..."

"A bed?" he suggested.

"Right you are. So what would you think of getting a head start on the festivities?"

He took her by the hand and led her into the bedroom. In the first pale light of dawn he slipped her robe off her shoulders and lifted her onto the bed.

"Jesse," he said softly. "It's really you, you and me together, the way it used to be." He bent and kissed her, his lips on hers as soft as a breeze.

"It really is," she replied, reaching up to slip her arms around his neck.

And as the night waned, Jack made love to her and said all the things she'd been pining to hear, satisfying her soul as fully as he had always satisfied her body.

Jessica woke later to a pale wintry day and a new life. The recent snowfall had left a layer of creamy frosting on everything she could see from the bedroom window, and she sat up to get a better look. It was amazing how, for the first time, she didn't mind waking up alone. She was confident that Jack was nearby and slid off the edge of the bed, belting her robe around her, to go look for him.

He was sitting near the window in the living room, wearing only a pair of jeans, staring out at the falling snow. An outside streetlamp, still on, cast a glow upon his face, and by its light Jessica could see the wetness of tears on his cheeks. He was crying.

She coughed loudly, making a production of shutting the door to the bedroom, giving him a chance to recover. She saw him wipe his eyes hastily with the back of his hand, and she waited until he motioned her closer before she went to him.

"What are you doing out here?" she asked him, perching on the arm of his chair and bending down to put her arms around his neck, resting her head against his shoulder.

"Thinking," he said. His voice sounded congested, nasal.

"About what?"

"About you."

"What about me?"

He shook his head. "I can't believe you put up with me acting like such a jerk all this time and never told me the truth."

"Jack, let's not talk about it anymore," she said wearily. "It's over and done with. I just want to forget it."

"I can't dismiss it that easily," he said huskily. "All I've done the past few years, all my plans and schemes, were based on a lie. I *lived* to get back at you, and it was all for nothing."

Jessica stood up, walked a few steps away and then turned to face him.

"If I had told you the truth ten years ago, you would have gone to jail. If I had told you the truth two months ago, you would have disgraced my family. I had to wait until your desire for revenge ran its course." She sighed. "I was beginning to think it never would."

He hung his head. "I am so sorry," he said hoarsely. He gave a short bark of laughter. "The words are pathetically inadequate, aren't they?"

Jessica returned to him and climbed into his lap. "Jack, I know you're sorry," she whispered. "Let's put it behind us and start over, now, today."

He stroked her hair, his voice rumbling in his chest as he said, "Jesse, I never touched Daphne after you came back to town. I swear it."

"Shush, darling, don't worry about that. It doesn't matter anymore."

"It does to me."

Jessica lifted her head and looked into his face. "Come back to bed and get a couple of hours' sleep before you go to work," she said.

"I can't sleep," he said tiredly. "I tried."

"Then just come lay down and rest," she coaxed, getting up and taking his hand, pulling him after her. He allowed her to lead him and then stretched out on the bed with a grateful sigh as she curled up next to him.

"I won't sleep," he said drowsily, his eyes closing.

"I know," Jessica agreed, smiling to herself. She waited until he was breathing evenly, and then relaxed into slumber as well, her arm flung protectively across his chest.

They both slept until noon. After lunch Jack dressed sheepishly to go to his office, knotting his tie before the bedroom mirror as Jessica hovered in the background, grinning at him.

"Kind of a late start for the boss to be getting, isn't it?" she asked, tapping him on the shoulder.

"Very funny. You were the one who shut off the alarm, as I recall," he replied, meeting her eyes in the glass.

"You didn't even hear it!" she hooted, laughing.

"Well, if I had," he observed piously, "I certainly wouldn't have shut it off." He turned and grabbed her, nuzzling her neck. "I will be home at precisely five-thirty," he announced. "What's for dinner?"

"You just had lunch."

"I believe in planning ahead."

"You don't even know if I can cook."

"You told me you could."

"Oh. Well, how does veal marsala sound?"

"It sounds great. What is it?"

"Veal."

"Thank you."

"Well, that's all it is, with a few extras thrown in."

"I see," he said equably, unbuttoning her blouse.

"Jack."

"Yes?"

"You'll never get to the office this way."

"You're right," he said, holding both of his hands in the air in a gesture of surrender. She stepped away from him as he picked up his jacket and coat and said, "Five-thirty."

She nodded.

He kissed her forehead. "Goodbye."

"Bye."

He turned in the doorway and said, "Veal marsala, huh?"

"You bet."

"Make it five o'clock," he amended, and went through the door.

Jessica spent the afternoon in a fever of preparations, running around to the stores to get all the things for dinner, humming and talking to herself like a bag lady. When she arrived back at the apartment, staggering under a load of paper sacks, the light was blinking on the answering machine. She pressed the button and Jack's voice announced, "I love you."

There were four more messages with the same content. She chuckled, turned off the machine and went to the kitchen to begin preparing the meal.

By the time Jack was due to arrive the apartment was filled with the heavenly aroma of veal sauteed in wine, and Jessica was bustling about, putting the finishing touches on the table. She couldn't help comparing this occasion with the first time she had planned such a dinner, but then dismissed the recollection. Today she only had room for happy thoughts.

When she heard Jack coming she whipped off her apron and stationed herself in the hallway to wait. The door opened, and a gigantic bunch of red roses preceded Jack into the room.

"For me?" she said, relieving him of the gaudy, fragrant burden.

"Yes, for you," he replied, kissing her and taking off his coat. "The florist was delighted. I bought out his stock." He sniffed enthusiastically. "Smells terrific."

"It's just about ready," Jessica said, putting the flowers in a vase. As she turned to face him he slipped his arm around her waist and kissed her deeply, running his hand up her thigh under her skirt. There was silence for about half a minute and then he said thickly, "Do you think it can wait?"

"What? The food?"

"Um-hmm." He was pulling her blouse loose from her waistband with his other hand.

"Jack, I don't know," she began, and then he slipped his fingers into the cup of her bra and stroked her breast.

"I guess so," she amended breathlessly.

An hour later Jessica rolled over in bed, remembered the congealing veal, and mentally said the hell with it. Jack was dozing with the sheet curled down to his waist, exposing the muscular expanse of his torso.

"Hey, Jacques," she said softly, nudging his bare shoulder. "Still here?"

He opened one eye. "Yup."

"Going anywhere?"

"Nope," he said, closing the eye again.

"Good." She sighed, settling down contentedly. He kissed her hair as he pulled her tight against him, and they both went back to sleep.

Take 4 Silhouette Intimate Moments novels
FREE

Then preview 4 brand new Silhouette Intimate Moments® novels —delivered to your door every month—for 15 days as soon as they are published. When you decide to keep them, you pay just $2.25 each ($2.50 each, in Canada), *with no shipping, handling, or other charges of any kind!*

Silhouette Intimate Moments novels are not for everyone. They were created to give you a more detailed, more exciting reading experience, filled with romantic fantasy, intense sensuality, and stirring passion.

The first 4 Silhouette Intimate Moments novels are absolutely FREE and without obligation, yours to keep. You can cancel at any time.

You'll also receive a FREE subscription to the Silhouette Books Newsletter as long as you remain a member. Each issue is filled with news on upcoming titles, interviews with your favorite authors, even their favorite recipes.

To get your 4 FREE books, fill out and mail the coupon today!

❀ *Silhouette Intimate Moments*®

Silhouette Books, 120 Brighton Rd., P.O. Box 5084, Clifton, NJ 07015-5084

**Clip and mail to: Silhouette Books,
120 Brighton Road, P.O. Box 5084, Clifton, NJ 07015-5084***

YES. Please send me 4 FREE Silhouette Intimate Moments novels. Unless you hear from me after I receive them, send me 4 brand new Silhouette Intimate Moments novels to preview each month. I understand you will bill me just $2.25 each, a total of $9.00 (in Canada, $2.50 each, a total of $10.00)—with no shipping, handling, or other charges of any kind. There is no minimum number of books that I must buy, and I can cancel at any time. The first 4 books are mine to keep. *Silhouette Intimate Moments available in Canada through subscription only.*   B1MS87

Name	(please print)

Address	Apt. #

City	State/Prov.	Zip/Postal Code

* In Canada, mail to: Silhouette Canadian Book Club,
320 Steelcase Rd., E., Markham, Ontario, L3R 2M1, Canada   IM-SUB-1B
Terms and prices subject to change.
SILHOUETTE INTIMATE MOMENTS is a service mark and registered trademark.

# Silhouette Desire

COMING NEXT MONTH

FIT FOR A KING—Diana Palmer
Elissa Dean was exactly who King Roper needed to protect him from his sister-in-law's advances. The act seemed foolproof... until Elissa's very presence set King's heart on fire.

DEAR READER—Jennifer Greene
Leslie Stuart needed to teach Sam Pierce, the country's leading mathematician, to overcome his dyslexia. But could he teach her to trust in his love?

LOVE IN THE AIR—Nan Ryan
More than the airwaves crackled whenever Sullivan and Kay signed on at station Q102. But after having left once before, Kay had to convince Sullivan that her heart was there to stay.

A PLACE TO BELONG—Christine Flynn
Rachel Summers and Eric Johnston needed each other. As a sports therapist, she had six weeks to bring this pro hockey player back into tip-top shape—just long enough to fall in love.

STILL WATERS—Leslie Davis Guccione
Another bride for a Branigan brother! You met Drew in BITTERSWEET HARVEST (Desire #311)—now Ryan Branigan and his childhood sweetheart reclaim their chance for love.

LADY ICE—Joan Hohl
Cool businesswoman Patricia Lycaster promised herself she'd be Peter Vanzant's wife in name only. But the more she resisted, the more determined he was to fan the desire that blazed between them.

AVAILABLE THIS MONTH:

BRIGHT RIVER
Doreen Owens Malek

BETTING MAN
Robin Elliott

COME FLY WITH ME
Sherryl Woods

CHOCOLATE DREAMS
Marie Nicole

GREAT EXPECTATIONS
Amanda Lee

SPELLBOUND
Joyce Thies

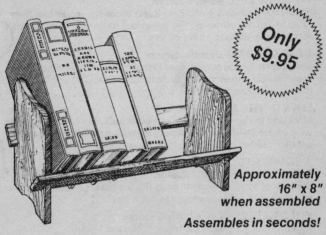